At Night She Cries,

WHILE HE RIDES HIS STEED

At Night She Cries,

WHILE HE RIDES HIS STEED

A Romance Novel for Dudes

ROSS PATTERSON

Regan Arts.

**Regan
Arts.**

65 Bleecker Street
New York, NY 10012

First Regan Arts hardcover edition, June 2015

Library of Congress Control Number: 2014955548

ISBN 978-1-941393-49-9

Interior design and background illustrations by Daniel Lagin
Jacket design by Richard Ljoenes
Jacket art and interior illustrations by Tim McDonagh

Printed in the United States of America

10   9   8   7   6   5   4   3   2   1

For Emma, Forever Ago.

Wait, that's the title of a fucking Bon Iver album.

For Nikki, my waitress at the Daytona Beach Hooters who I had sex with and never called back. I knew shit was going down when you drew hearts instead of dotting the *i*'s in your name on my receipt. In case I left you with child, this book is for you. Also, if you want to fake my signature on it and give it to him or her like it came from me, feel free. I won't say shit.

Contents

CONTENTS

CONTENTS

The Life of St. James St. James

As I sit at an aged wooden table at the back of Manhattan's oldest bar, a man walks in and demands a Michelob Ultra. The bartender shakes his head and replies, "We only have two types of beer here, light and dark. We also never had to serve women until a court order in 1970."

The guy looks at him incredulously and says, "I *am* a man."

"Not if you're ordering *a fucking Michelob Ultra!*" I shake my head and laugh to myself as the man walks out. It's only fitting that I'm doing this here.

Hello, I'm Saint James Street James. I hate road abbreviations, so I spell out my last name. At some point in your life you've seen me partying all over the world, gracing the covers of many famous sport-fishing and leisure magazines over the years—along with my twenty-six-page spread in the infamous July 1973 issue of *Playgirl* that's been banned, except in Luxembourg. You may think you already know everything about me, but you don't. The one secret I've been harboring for most of my adult life is . . . *that I'm 186 years old.* That's not a misprint, I'm 1-8-6, holmes. Yeah, I put an *L* in "homes" so you would understand how serious I am.

I was rich enough to almost triple my life expectancy, while permanently maintaining the looks of a thirty-five-year-old man still in his prime. Oh, and I also beat AIDS. *Twice.* You can do that shit when you're rich, and I am *really* fucking rich. The only other way to beat AIDS is if you win the Olympics. Go ask Magic Johnson or Greg Louganis if you don't believe me.

Why am I telling you this? After living 186 years on this planet, I've become bored—and unless a scientist invents a new place to put a hole in a woman, I've done everything else there is to do in this life. I'm also tired of seeing what the male species has evolved into, so the moment I finish writing my memoirs about my life . . . I'm going to off myself. You read that correctly, *I'm going to kill myself.* This isn't going to be a casual Paris Jackson "I ate a bunch of children's chewy Tylenol" suicide attempt; I'm going to blow my fucking brains out.

Before I do, I want you to know the real truth about me. That's why I'm writing this book with nothing but a loaded handgun and a pile of freshly cut pure Bolivian cocaine next to my old classic Remington Rand typewriter that Hemingway gave me. He only used it once, as a urinal at a house party. After relieving himself, he shook twice and typed only one sentence on a piece of paper: "This typewriter smells like piss; get a new one, fuckface." Classic Hemingway.

If all of this sounds too intense, then stop reading the rest of this shit right now. Seriously, put down your glasses without the prescription in them and close this book, because this kind of male hubris isn't for you. I'm not going to apologize for being a real man, and I certainly don't know when it became trendy to tell everyone that "you weren't cool in high school."

Back in 1827 I was born in a time when men were actually *men*. We fucked whoever we wanted, whenever we wanted, we didn't pull out, and the only "child support" that was given was if you put a blanket in the basket before you dropped your illegitimate baby off on a stranger's front porch. We didn't cook shit using Pam or butter, just a raw skillet, and maybe a little spit. We put our boxers on backward so we could take a shit without having to pull them down before we sat down in an outhouse.

The following memoir is filled with the most important stories ever told in the history of the United States. It will end all stories about every other man ever told, so go fuck yourself, Buzz Aldrin. Enjoy my life.

—Sincerely, St. James St. James

Chapter One

MONDAY, APRIL 30, 1849— COLOMA, CALIFORNIA: THE DAY THAT I BECAME RICH

A tall, thirty-two-year-old man stares deep inside a filthy hellhole of a gold mine with a dimly lit lantern, trying to see through a cloud of dust. This man is me, but I refuse to give any further physical description of myself until I'm wealthy. Most great men usually do. What I can tell you is that I'm jammed between the tits of the great American gold rush of 1849, and shit is fucking real. This isn't a goddamn hobby where you take your kid out panning for gold with a spaghetti strainer on Sundays hoping for the best. People have died doing this. Which is why I pay someone else to do it for me.

Suddenly a dirty Chinaman in his forties emerges from the dark hole with three dead parrots clinging to his shirt. He's smiling through cracked "dying of thirst" lips, but my eyes are fixated on his tiny, yellow hand. I don't want him touching me, so I shine my lantern in his face and demand that he stop walking toward me.

Dropping to his knees, he cries out, "You rich, boss. You rich!"

He opens his hand to reveal a small, brightly speckled rock covered in mud. I make him take off one of his wooden shoes and place the pebble inside it. Carefully, I remove the canteen from around my neck and wash the dirt away. It appears to be gold, but to be sure, I make him bite into it.

Staring at the nugget nervously, he knows what he has to do. He closes his eyes, places the nugget into his mouth, and bites down hard. Instead of his rotting teeth breaking off instantly, they make a soft imprint. Holy. Fucking. Shit. It's real hardcore American gold, and I'm fucking rich.

I won't bore you with the details of how I then made this Chinaman excavate and load 480 pounds of gold onto my wagon, drag it into town personally (because I didn't want to tire out my horse), and melt it down into gold bars by hand while I stood behind him with a loaded shotgun pointed at his head. Come to think of it, that was probably only boring for me—he was probably scared shitless.

On that note, congratulations, you've just read the best first chapter of any book ever written. Notice how I skipped over my childhood and all that bullshit? That's because nothing cool happens in your life until you become rich, and up until the moment you just read about, I was a poor-ass farmer. My parents were decent people, but they were working-class citizens, whose only claim to fame was that former president Martin Van Buren once took a shit in our outhouse during a campaign visit to California. You sure as fuck didn't pay fifteen bucks to read about that. Let's just get to me being rich and fucking awesome. You're welcome.

Chapter Two

BEING RICH MAKES YOU
A BETTER PERSON

July 19, 1853—four years later. An extremely muscular man with calves and forearms that have more definition than Noah Webster's dictionary busts through the saloon doors of a tasteful whorehouse with a burlap sack full of gold slung over his shoulder. The doors explode off their hinges into a shower of splinters. The surprising thing about this muscular man is that he is lean too, not all 'roided out like a New Jersey teenager triple-stacking a month before spring break. You can see his cock pressing hard against his jeans, almost fighting with the left pant leg, mid-thigh. It's not like the jeans are super tight or have some kind of Euro cut, it's just how big his penis is. This man is me, Saint James Street James, and this is now the description I deserve.

I survey the whorehouse-slash-bar through squinted eyes—eyes so beautiful, butterflies masturbate after looking into them. Every whore in the entire place falls to her knees and prays toward me like I'm a Mayan god. I raise my hand, acknowledging them.

"Let me get a drink first, whores. Remember, sleeping with me is a privilege, not a right. So I'll obviously be going by looks again today."

"If he doesn't make love to me *right now*, I'll fucking kill myself!" one screams as she presses a knife forcefully into her neck.

"Grandma, stop it! You're acting fucking crazy!" her granddaughter says as she tackles her to the ground. Another whore races in and kicks the knife out of her hand as the grandma begins convulsing and speaking in tongues.

You give these whores an inch, they want the other seven. Unfazed, I walk up to the bar and take a seat. I drop my large burlap sack of gold on the floor and groan heavily, letting everyone in the saloon know who the fuck I am. The weight of the gold causes several floorboards to break, and a few whores faint.

I yell out to the man behind the bar, who is inches in front of my face: "Quietly hand me an entire bottle of fucking whiskey, and be discreet about it!"

An old Indian bartender in his fifties, Manuel, stares at me, exasperated. "You're going to have to pay for those double doors you broke first, Saint James."

I exhale in his face for fifty-eight seconds straight without blinking, just to prove a point. He doesn't blink once, and neither do I. This is our little game. He used to work on our farm and babysit me as a kid. We would play cowboys and Indians, except we weren't pretending. I consider him the closest thing I have to a "friend" in this town, but men never let that shit show back then. So instead, I reach into my burlap sack and pull out a large chunk of gold and drop it on top of the bar.

"Here you go, fuckface. Bottle me up."

Without a hint of "non," I *chalantly* slide my hand into my full-length elk-skin duster and whistle a show tune with pitch-perfect precision. I tap the exposed handle of my six-shooter, which is peeking out from my gun holster, hip-high, and begin counting aloud how long it takes him to get me a drink in numerical "Mississippis." Manuel shakes his head as he puts a bottle and a shot glass down in front of me. I wave him off.

"I'm gonna go ahead and grab the whole tit, so you can hold off on putting that training bra on, Manuel."

He nods and removes the shot glass from the bar. I take a long swig and eye a couple of the whores. Subtlety does *not* ensue, and I stick my entire tongue inside the bottle to make sure they know what I want. One whore blushes, as she continues to jack off a random man underneath a table. He gets caught up in my whole shit and tries to make eye contact with me. Even dudes want to be inside me.*

A buck-naked man suddenly walks through the hole left by the missing saloon doors, wearing only his cowboy boots. He throws a horse saddle on the ground.

"A goddamn grizzly ate all my clothes off. Can I get a ride to New Mexico to get my other pair of pants?"

---

* The only man who had the kind of sexual power that I've had over the last century was George Washington Carver. Imagine smelling like a fresh bag of peanuts in every room you walked into. Carver knew it, utilized his strengths, and turned out more tricks than Criss Angel. He was pimp like that.

In record time, I unholster my gun and shoot him in the chest. His body goes flying out of the saloon with his dick and balls slamming back against his abdomen. It happens so quickly that it ends up being a double-tap. It's not like I am staring hard, I just have the hearing of a dolphin. That double-tap sound is so distinct.

"Jesus, Saint James, you just shot New Mexico Mike!"

"That motherfucker comes in here like that once a week, and I'm sick of it."

"It's casual Friday," he says solemnly as he cleans a glass.

"Is it? Sorry, Manny. I always forget."

Two Indian bar backs scurry out and pull Mike by his legs across the floor and out the back door. In memory of Mike, I down the rest of my bottle of whiskey, then proceed to chug an entire bottle that rests in front of a stranger sitting next to me.

I stand up and smash both bottles off my flexed traps and scream in no particular direction: "I need three whores! Two of them must have some type of background or formal training in circus 'performantry,' and the other must be able to throw twice her body mass above her head."

Within seconds, I feel a tap on my shoulder, and turn to see three eager women standing in a perfect pyramid directly behind me.

"I guess you'll do," I say, before pushing them over on the floor and walking back to a shitty makeshift bedroom. When I hit the door of the bedroom, I loudly clear my throat, looking back at the whores.

"I said, '*I guess you'll do!*' Get up off the floor and have some respect for yourselves."

All three whores run toward the bedroom like I just announced

I had a cure for smallpox. A weird man holding a live chicken stands next to the bedroom, and I punch him directly in the dick for looking at me the wrong way. He falls down in front of me, and I step over him as if he doesn't exist. The chicken scampers away as he holds his junk, writhing on the floor in anguish.

"I wasn't looking at you the wrong way, I was born cross-eyed!" the man screams.

Turns out he really is cross-eyed. I don't bother apologizing, though; I'm sure he gets that all the time. What am I going to do about it now, *not* fuck these girls? You can't hear it, but laughter is coming out of my mouth as I write this.

After the whores race in, I slam the bedroom door and begin to pull off my pants, peeling them down to the top of my boots. I sit down in an old wooden rocking chair in the corner of the room, take a cigarette out of my duster jacket, and strike a match off my right boot, which is now awkwardly pulled up above my dong. The spark of the match lights up the room, and after lighting my cigarette I use the remaining flame to light a small lantern on the nightstand next to me. All three women are now magically lit as if they're sitting for a presidential portrait.

Even in soft, intimate lighting, I can clearly see that two of the whores are sixes on their best day; the other is a firm four. You can do the math yourself, but that is way past a ten total, so don't fucking judge me. *I'm at a whorehouse in Coloma, California, in 1853.* Trust me when I say that we are lucky to have sixes.

I smile as I look down at myself. "Well, dick, it's up to you now; I drank two bottles of whiskey and killed a dude, now you need to do the fucking." My dick nods at me. We have a long, storied history together.

"Will you please take your boots off? We would be honored," one of the hotter ones says.

Having heard this sentence a thousand times before, I laugh in her face. "I know you would, but I'm married. Let's just get undressed and not pretend that this might turn into something eventually."

If a married man takes his boots off to have sex with prostitutes, it's cheating. If he doesn't, he's just blowing off steam and banging whores. The whores know that, yet they always want something more. "Oh, you've had sex with over four hundred grimy fucking miners, will you marry me?" I promise that thought wouldn't be on my mind throughout the rest of our wedded bliss. Hilarious.

"What do you want us to do?" the larger whore asks.

"Honestly, you are definitely the spotter of the group—I'd like you to just shut the fuck up and be the best base you can be. Don't drop the two hotter girls or make direct eye contact with me. And please don't ask if you can get boned by me too."

She nods, obviously knowing her place in life. Inhaling deeply, she braces her fingers together to form a "handbasket" for the others to climb into. One at a time, the two other girls place a foot inside her clasped hands, and she expertly flips each one of them onto the bed. The execution and landing are perfect. I applaud quietly and hop over to the bed with my pants still down around my ankles* to join the other two.

---

* No, I never pulled my jeans off over my boots to fuck. That would require too much effort. Remember, these are just random whores.

As the women strip down, I whistle at the two hot ones and smash my index fingers together—signaling the international sign for "You two make out." They oblige. What happens next is a sexual tornado involving one man, two women, and the girl who was always the first out in "dodge rock."

By the way, just because I fuck with my boots on, don't think for one goddamn second it limits me sexually in any way. Truth be told, it makes me experiment more, because I have to be more creative. To prove it, I start off by blindfolding each of them and making them grab the headboard. This way my dick is truly a surprise, and the one not being dicked always wonders when her turn is coming—and more important, for how long. I switch up my rhythms, knowing their confusion mixed with blindness is something that only Helen Keller or every blind person ever has probably experienced.

When I am behind one woman, I use my fingers to play the other woman's lady hole with the precision of a cellist. As I repeatedly switch back and forth between the two girls with a complex rhythm, the bigger one conducts her own two-finger symphony in the corner, per my instructions. I'm on some real Beethoven shit tonight. My mastery of sex has turned into an impromptu concerto, with four people playing as one, each giving everything they have, knowing full well it is for the best of the group. You're only as good as your instrument, and on this night, I am finely tuned.

After the whores have thirty-eight and a half orgasms collectively, I finally decide that it's my turn to grab a gift from under the Christmas tree. Right before I climax, I grab a Buck knife still strapped to my calf, along with the bedsheet that has long ago been pulled off. I toss them to the big girl in the corner and make circular motions with my fingers, instructing her what to do. Once it clicks in, she knows exactly the surprise I have in store for these ladies.

With my last thrust, just as I am peaking, I pull off each of the girls' blindfolds at the same time. The big girl runs around the side of the bed, now wearing the bedsheet as a ghost costume.

"Boo, motherfuckers!" she screams at the girls.

Terror-stricken, the two women slap each other simultaneously in the face as hard as they can and fall to the bed. Imagine the first thing you see after an hour and a half of intense blindfolded sex is a giant ghost shaking her hands in your face. To the big one's credit, the eyeholes she cut out in the sheet are flawless. She must have been a seamstress before whoring, because typically you don't find tailoring like that. Good for her—it's always nice for people to have an extra skill.

After I pull up my jeans, I remove my timepiece and exhale deeply. Time to go home to the wife and kids for supper. I wipe my face with a pillowcase and drop two large chunks of gold down on the nightstand before I leave. The overweight one obviously gets nothing. I look back to admire my handiwork and see the two hot girls lying on the bed like an exorcism just happened, while the fat ghost waves good-bye to me.

When I walk out, I'm greeted by thunderous applause from the entire bar. The walls are super thin; I knew it, and they appreciate the performance I just put on in there. I throw the pillowcase into the crowd as a souvenir, and whores begin fighting over it. My steed runs into the bar, and on cue, two gimpy patrons lift me up into the saddle. I sling my burlap sack full of gold over my shoulder and ride out through the hole left by the broken double doors in a championship exit.

Chapter Three

IT'S HARD TO GET THE SMELL OF SEX OFF

I feel more worn out than a stepladder in a midget's kitchen as I ride up to my three-story log cabin. Remember, I'm really fucking rich, so this goddamn place looks like a Norman Rockwell painting having a ménage with *A River Runs Through It* and *Legends of the Fall*. Even though it's enormous, I only put in fourteen bedrooms to keep things tasteful. My legs feel wobbly when I dismount. I'm not sure if it's from the graphic sex I've just had, or the six-mile ride home from the bar. I lead my horse to the large, beautiful river that flows in front of my home.

"Drink, fucker."

As he leans down to drink, I kneel down beside him and splash some water on my dick and balls to get the smell of pussy off me. When the sex water drifts downstream and reaches his snout, my horse smiles at me as if to say, "You fucking son of a bitch! Why didn't you let me peek in the window? I'm a horse—they wouldn't have suspected anything weird."

I remember thinking at the time, "My steed and I *are* close; maybe I should let him watch sometime." I've never lost wood before, and I've done some sick shit. I definitely wouldn't lose a boner just because a horse is in the room.

From my back pocket I pull out a handkerchief emblazoned with the initials "SJSJ" in 14 karat gold, and wipe off my dong. Then I throw it in the water because I hate *used* shit. As I watch it float away, I see a huge, bright full moon reflecting off the water, smiling down. It winks at me, and we share a nice moment. I take my gun out of the holster and fire it into the air.

"Children, your father is home!"

I lumber toward the house with my sack full of gold. Upon walking in, I see my thirty-two-year-old wife, Louretta, a tall, redheaded Irish woman with huge tits. Also staring up at me respectfully are my seven boys, all under the age of eight. Each one of them tightens his hungry fists, gripping forks and knifes. They all begin chanting in unison, "We want gold! We want gold! We want gold!"

Louretta smiles and shrugs her shoulders. "What do you expect, they're starving. They've been waiting for you to get home."

"I can't be *that* late for dinner. What time is it?"

"It's two-thirty in the morning."

"Oh. Sorry. I thought this was one of those fall-back time-change days."

She rolls her eyes and hands me a metal cheese grater. I pull out a chunk of gold and begin to lightly shred it over my boys' plates of meat and potatoes. They tear into their cold dinners like tiny Viking warriors. Satisfied that they've each gotten enough, I give the rest of my chunk of gold to my youngest, Bourbon Street James, who is one year old. He claps excitedly and puts it in his mouth, sucking on it.

Exhausted, I pull up a chair and look down at the faces of my children. As a man, there is no bigger satisfaction than coming home with a huge sack of gold every night, and hearing the sounds of your children's teeth chomping into our country's best nonrenewable natural resource. I kick my boots up on the table and light up a cigarette as Louretta brings me my ashtray that's made out of half a monkey skull that I won in a poker match in Reno. I'm not even sure whose monkey it was, I just thought it would be a good conversation starter if we had people over. Taking a drag of my smoke, I watch Louretta walk back to the kitchen to clean dishes. I whistle at her, but she doesn't smile back.

"Pigtits, can you draw me a hot bath after you're done in there? I'm exhausted from another long day of standing over my Chinaman and watching him dig my gold."

She stares at me incredulously before finally replying, "I'm going to have to boil like forty-eight pots of hot water to do that right now."

"Awesome, thanks, doll, you're a lamb of God." I fire a pretend six-shooter at her with my fingers.

As she storms off, I look over at my kids and ask, "How was your day?"

My oldest son, Daniel, who is almost eight, speaks up. "It was so much—

"Rhetorical," I say, cutting him off.

They're seven kids under the age of eight who go to a bullshit schoolhouse that holds eighteen children total. All they learn is how to read and count on their fingers. Big fucking deal. After I finish my cigarette, boredom sets in, and I whistle for Louretta as I walk upstairs into the bedroom.

"Bath time, Red. Let's start filling up those pots. I can't wash myself."

When Louretta finally hobbles in twenty minutes later with two pots of boiling water, I'm already stark-ass naked, stretched out inside my personal claw-foot tub that is also made out of 14 karat gold. A large, golden grizzly bear head is mounted to the front of the tub, facing inward.

"Are ya comfortable?" she asks.

"Not really. Let's put a rush on that water, Ginge. I don't want it to be *too* hot, then *too* cold. You get it."

She splashes both pots of semi-warm water on me, and storms out. This goes on for the next hour or so until she finally limps in with the last two pots, her arms shaking from the effort. I stare at her like a nervous parent at the Special Olympics as she slowly walks over to the tub and pours them in. I clap for her when she finishes, then hold up a bar of soap and lean forward, pointing at my back. She drops to her knees and begins to scrub my back and genitals. On my jennies, I'm not talking about washing them from the front, but from behind and up underneath—the way God intended them to be scrubbed.

"Do you want to get in this tub with me?" I ask Louretta.

"No. I just want to get some sleep. The kids have to be up in five hours, and I'm exhausted."

"Jesus, you're a fucking downer. Now do you understand why I'm always late for dinner? You're always asking me to help with the kids, crying about your sister's polio, or asking me to send letters back to your family members in Ireland to see if they're still alive after the potato famine. I'm not a fucking postman or someone whose biggest fault is that 'they listen *too* much.' I'm a real fucking man . . . who needs a power wash with those two." I point at her breasts.*

"Is that all I am to you?" she asks, choked up.

"Don't be so hard on yourself. You also cook and clean too."

"It's nice to know that's what you think of me."

Louretta breaks down and starts to cry, so I rub her back with my hand, then expertly pop her bra off. "Come on, Lou, don't be like that. If you didn't clean me, I would be dirty as fuck."

She shakes her head in disbelief at how awesome I am, giving me the old "this is the last time" look, as she slowly removes her top. Her breasts escape from her bra with the desperation of *two* Anne Franks, both wanting to see the outside world. I'm continuously amazed at how enormous her areolas are. They take up such a wide area of her breast, it's like seeing the tarp covering the infield during a rain delay at a ball game.

Ever so delicately, she pulls down the rest of her dress, revealing

---

* A power wash is when a woman with huge breasts soaps them up and washes you with them in a back-and-forth motion with enough power to kill a small elk.

an ass like a honey-glazed Christmas ham freshly cut down the center, and an unbelievable bush. If you don't have enough club, you're going to have trouble making it to the green from that rough. She doesn't say anything to me as she steps into the tub—her eyes entranced in a catatonic stare. I reach up and put my hand on her breast.

"Do you not like this?" I ask in a German accent, just because I can do one.

"I know where you've been tonight. Just do what you're going to do."

"Sshhhhhh. Once I get going, you'll forget about all the other women I've slept with and appreciate the new techniques I've learned."

She finally shows a hint of a smile, acknowledging the fact that she's able to reach sexual heights with me that she could never achieve with another man. As she straddles me and begins to ride me, water splashes up over the sides of the tub and onto the floor. Her massive breasts have caused a tsunami-like current, creating the kind of deep curls that Kelly Slater deuces his wet suit over. I whistle softly, inviting my steed over to peek in the window. He nods at me with appreciation for the heads-up as he trots over and sticks his head in.

I was right—I'm definitely not losing wood over it. If anything, I've gained an extra inch. As much as I'm proud of myself at this moment, I'm even prouder of my dick, which has been through fucking war today. I let Louretta's slow ride continue for a few more minutes, but I'm already mentally planning my ground strategy. Why? *Because I hate having sex in water.*

Having sex in the water is like dry-humping in button-fly jeans. It's awkward, it hurts, and you can't feel anything. Don't get me wrong, it's a decent hors d'oeuvre, like a bacon-wrapped plantain, but it's no Awesome Blossom when it comes to starter apps. If shit is going to get live, you need to do it on dry land so you can get some real traction—feet, elbows, knees—any kind of grip. I squeeze her ass cheeks hard and lift her up out of the water, creating one last, final tidal wave that pushes the rest of the bathwater out of the tub underneath the bedroom door.

"Hold my hand, I'm not going to lose you in this!" one of my kids screams out to the other children.

"The current is too strong! This is probably where we say good-bye!" another answers.

"Shut the fuck up! We're making love in here!" I scream.

Hearing a child's voice during lovemaking would usually make most men lose an erection, but I'm not most men. I'm Saint James Street James, so I walk over to the closest full-length mirror in our bedroom to purposefully catch a glimpse of myself wet and fully flexed, which fuels my fire. I'm cut like a fresh London broil after Sunday mass. Nothing gets me harder than being able to see myself during sex.

When I rise up on my tiptoes three inches so I can see every last goddamn tendon in my calf muscles swell, Louretta becomes suspicious, and I'm forced to turn my attention back toward her. There were still a few more poses I wanted to beast out, but that will have to wait for another day. Instead, I carry Louretta over to the bed as she holds out her arms. She braces them as if I'm going to drop her down aggressively, but I don't.

Instead, I flip her upside down and go for the standing-up 69. It's a move seldom used or even seen for that matter, and truthfully I don't even know if I'm doing it for me, or just to impress my horse. It requires so much upper-body strength that hopefully it throws my wife off the trail of how much sex I *actually* had earlier. Who else could do this right now? Off the top of my head, Jesus or Zeus maybe? After that I'm blanking.*

After thirty minutes of standing cunnilingus, I rotate her right-side up and toss her backward onto the bed like a Romanian acrobat. We begin to make love passionately on the bed in the missionary position. By now you probably notice that I keep saying "making love" when referring to my wife. It's because she's my fucking wife, asshole, so I don't treat her the same as the other whores. My seven children came out of her vagina—all of them through natural childbirth—and I respect that shit. The least I can do is make love to her.

After her *second* orgasm, I flip her over on top of me, cowgirl style. I leave the lanterns on in the room so I can see her huge natural tits swinging back and forth off her chest. With her on top, I can finally go full-bone and get every single last inch in.

As I thrust, I lean forward, slightly raising my upper body off the

---

* I'm putting Jesus in the same sentence as me out of respect, but truthfully I don't see him balling out like me.

bed so my abdominal muscles can be on full display. Louretta deserves this. Nay, she *needs* this.

"Do you have any laundry you need to do? Otherwise, I'll put this washboard away."

"No, not yet. You better keep it out."

She starts punching me in the stomach repeatedly as she keeps riding. I begin doing a series of mini ab crunches, just because it feels right. After a clean set of forty, and two more orgasms had by her, it's time for me to climax. I've never been accused of being a selfish lover—some might even say that I give *too much* of myself in the bedroom—so my orgasm is well deserved at this point. It's time to downgrade this Cat 5 boner to a tropical storm.

"Make them spin like cows caught in a tornado," I say softly.

She nods and leans back, rocking her ass back and forth on my dick and causing her tits to bang together like a wet seal clapping. It's times like these when I realize why I married her. She always had the biggest tits in town, and every man hated that she married me. By the way, these are the exact thoughts that go through my mind every time I climax. I also tend to think about revenge shit I'm going to do to other people. It's fucked up, but it somehow heightens my orgasms. Squeezing her apple-bottom ass, I arch my back and finally release.

"I'm achieving!" I scream out at the top of my lungs.

As that simple, two-word sentence flies out the window and echoes across the land, I look over and lock eyes with my steed, who stares at me with admiration. It's a moment of pure, utter bliss. Louretta crumbles on top of me and puts her head on my shoulder, looking up at me like a lost puppy dressed up as a wizard.

"Saint James, I've been thinking about something a lot today."

"That you want me to build a separate house for the children to live in so we don't ever have to hear them and they can raise themselves? I'm cool with that. I can have a crew of builders out here tomorrow."

"What? No!"

"Oh, then what is it?"

"I was thinking we could get a cat. The kids *really* want one."

"Why the fuck would you even ask me shit like that? A *cat*? Not in this fucking lifetime. All of our kids would be sucking each other's dicks the second that goddamn thing arrived. *Men. Don't. Have. Cats.* I'm going to go sleep in the barn with my steed. Thanks for ruining this moment."

I pull my arm out from under her so fast that her head barely moves from the pillow. Still buck naked, I get up and grab my jeans off the floor, and jumping straight up, in midair, I put them on *both* legs at a time. Using my foot, I grab my cowboy hat off the ground and flip it up onto my head as I leave. Louretta pulls the bedsheets up, covering herself as she quietly sobs.

"I just thought it would be nice," she says softly.

After I slam the bedroom door and leave, I notice my feet are wet. "Daniel, get a mop and clean up this bathwater in the living room! It's fucking soaked!"

Not one great man in history has ever owned a cat; therefore my sons never will. This is why I love my steed more than anything in this world—he would never do some shit like this. Ever.

That night, as I lie on the ground out in the barn with him curled up behind me, using his torso as my pillow, I dream of the day I first met him. I was a young boy, maybe seven or eight, when I saw him standing there on top of a diving platform at the Nevada State Fair. He must have been twelve stories up. There was this jackdick dressed in a tasseled cowboy outfit on top of him, rousing up the crowd with his ten-gallon hat.

"Who wants to see us jump into this unbelievably small pool of water below?" he screamed at the cheering crowd.

I sure as fuck didn't. That's when the horse and I locked eyes. I noticed his grace and beauty right away, plus I dug the fact that he wasn't afraid of heights. From that moment I knew that he needed to be my steed. After that split second of eye contact, he sensed what he had to do—kill the asshole riding him. Without warning, he leaped off the edge and did a triple backflip, throwing that fake, wannabe cowboy off him, way out past the crowd.

As all the people gasped in horror, that fringed asshole hit the ground with a collision so violent that his organs exploded out of his body. When the carnies rushed to attend to what was left of him, my steed climbed out of the pool and strode over to me. No one even noticed us ride off together, and we've never been apart since. You tell me that you've had a stronger relationship than that in your whole life, and I'll let you piss on my face sitting down.

Chapter Four

EVERY MAN NEEDS A DYNAMITE MONTAGE TO FEEL ALIVE

The warm sun shines down through the slats of the barn against the buttons on my jeans. It feels like my cock is being burned off, and I jolt upright. I wipe my eyes and notice a half bottle of whiskey near me. I take a swig to get the engines going, then pull down my pants and take a shit in the stall where my horse shits. Hard clumps hit the hay right next to his pile.

"Daniel, come clean out the fucking stable! There's shit all over it!"

"Damn it! Why is it always me, Dad?"

I stumble outside the barn and see four of my boys holding ladles, drinking out of a large trough full of water. Casually nudging them aside, I dunk my head in. Louretta comes running out of the house screaming at me so loudly I can physically hear her underwater.

"Saint James, that's the clean drinking water for the kids!"

"Goddamn it, woman, it's not like we don't have an entire river that runs right in front of our fucking house. I'm going out for the day."

I blow past her into the house, grabbing a shirt, my cowboy boots, and a large, overstuffed saddlebag by the front door. My steed comes running out of the barn with his saddle already on. One of my middle kids is on all fours in front of me, so I use his back to step up onto my horse.

"Dad, I was playing jacks!" my son says.

"You're welcome, buddy," I say as I begin to trot off. Looking back, I notice Daniel shaking his head as he shovels my shit out of the barn.

"This fucking stinks, Dad!" he says to me.

I look at him and say, "I tell you what, you go find some gold, then maybe you can come out and shit in the barn then tell someone else to clean it up. Deal?"

I salute everyone and ride off into the distance. It's days like these where I just need some time to myself to cool off and blow shit up. I need a fucking sweet dynamite montage. Hell, *every* man needs one.

Riding through the forest, I bear down on my steed while expertly holding a lit match in between my teeth, spotting my first target—a beautiful set of ten baby Christmas trees. I grab a stick of dynamite from my saddlebag, light it, and throw it behind my back no-look style.* The explosion uproots the trees, and they crash to the

---

* Yeah, I invented dynamite, not that other dickbag who has a peace prize named after him. It wasn't that fucking hard to figure out how to dump a bunch of gunpowder in something and light it.

ground. All I see is a few stumps smoldering as a dirt cloud shoots high up into the air.

Now that I'm in a rhythm, I see a large moose off to my left. I sky-hook a lit stick over my head—*boom!* That fucker explodes into a thousand pieces. Chunks of fur and blood are scattered all over the trees and my clothes. A set of moose teeth and one hoof are all that remain.

"Fuck yeah! I just did that!" I say to myself out loud.

After two hours of blowing shit up, I stop next to the river and jump down from my horse. I hear hunger pains from my steed, so I reach into my saddlebag and grab the last stick of dynamite.

"You hungry, buddy?"

He nods that he is. "Okay, okay. Stand back."

I light the final stick and casually toss it into the river. Trout and salmon explode out of the water and rain down from the sky in front of him. Typically, horses don't eat fish, but mine has Champagne tastes just like I do. He grins with a look of satisfaction on his face as I bend down and drink out of the river, which has resumed a proper flow. With the water rushing over my lips, something washes up and sticks to the side of my face. I lift my head up and peel what feels like wet cloth off my cheek.

Looking closely, I notice it's my SJSJ handkerchief from last night, except now there's a little blood on it. What the fuck? I unholster my guns and turn upstream, when all of the sudden—*boom!* The ground shakes beneath my feet, followed by men's laughter echoing down the mountain. My acute sense of hearing detects nine white males in their late thirties and early forties, and one Asian male whose age is unknown because our calendar system is different.

"Boss! You rich! You rich!" the Asian man screams.

Son of a bitch. More laughter echoes louder. I know exactly what this means, and it isn't good. Quickly, I holster back up and put my handkerchief in my pocket.

For good measure, I also pull a small mango out of my saddlebag, make an incision in it, squeeze all the juice into my mouth, and snort a key bump of gunpowder. This concoction is known as a Standing Jonathan. It gives me strength throughout my quads and keeps my mind sharp in case I have to kill a large group of people at the same time. My friend Pete Newhouse, who dabbled in homosexuality, invented it. Pete died a couple years later fighting for what he believed in: same-sex clothing for his wife. He always dressed her like a dude, and she killed him for it.

After pounding my Standing Jonathan, my mind is clearer than an albino's iris as I ride my steed toward the chaos and confusion. I wish this book had a trip wire for this page, so that when you read that last line—"ride my steed toward the chaos and confusion"—Mozart's *Requiem in D Minor* would kick in. Also, if a picture could pop out, of me with a huge boner, that would be dope too. I'll also settle for an illustration, just saying.

Riding up the side of the mountain, I come to a halt when I see an explosion inside a mining shaft, much like my own. A group of men stand around the mine's opening, and a small Asian man comes running out covered in dirt and mud. He's screaming and holding up a bloody piece of gold. Déjà vu hits me like a fist to my butthole.

"What do we have here, gentlemen?" I ask.

All the men turn at once and reach for their guns. I shoot the chunk of gold out of the Asian man's hand, taking off two of his fingers as well. That might seem extreme, but blowing off two of his fingers will later help me to distinguish my Asian from theirs, so it is kind of a two-birds thing. The men freeze as the Asian man screams in pain. Amazingly, they're hesitant to draw, even though it's nine against one. That's how fucking badass I am.

"We don't want no trouble," one of them says in a thick Southern accent.

"Okay. Then I want everyone to take off their pants and tell me what the fuck you're doing here."

As the men bend down and start to undress, one of them pipes up, "Why do we have to take off our pants?"

"In case one of you has any knives on you. I have fourteen knives strapped to various parts of my thighs and calves as we speak, but you can't see them, can you?"

Everyone shakes their heads no. Another man puts his hand up. "Hold up, boys. Nobody let their pants hit the ground. Are you the sheriff or something?"

The men pause, pants at mid-thigh.

"Some might call me the sheriff. I'm the richest man in town, so close enough."

The biggest and the oldest man laughs. He pulls up his pants and whistles with two fingers. Out of a makeshift tent in the distance behind him, a beautiful topless blonde woman with milkmaid braids rolls out a wheelbarrow full of gold. She looks like she just ran down the Swiss Alps through a perfect field of tits—that's how flawless she is.

My first thought is, "Holy shit, what if someone is richer than me? What will all the people in town think? Also, why didn't I think of hiring topless women for my gold mine? That's fucking genius." I snap out of it and regain my focus.

"Do you have a deed for this mine?" I ask.

"Yup," the big man says as he pulls a folded-up paper out of his pocket and approaches me. He sticks two fingers into his mouth and again whistles loudly. *Boom! Boom! Boom! Boom! Boom! Boom!* One by one, dynamite explodes inside too many mine shafts to count. As I duck my head, he smiles broadly. Half of his teeth are missing, the other half are gold.

"Also got deeds for the rest of 'em too."

The men all laugh in unison, exposing their gold teeth as well. A whole team of hot, topless Dutch women strut out of the tent on cue with empty wheelbarrows, rolling them to their respective mines. These guys are way more advanced than me. Also, these women are obviously 100 percent authentic European chicks. It isn't like they are haggard and suffered through hardships to escape oppression. They look *happy* to be doing this shit. Jesus Christ. I feel my world ending as my vision blurs, staring at the deeds. Somehow, I'm able to make out the name that's on all of them: the Schläger Bros. I've never heard of them.

"The Schläger Brothers? Where are you from, and how come I've never heard of you?"

"West Virginia originally, but we've been here almost two years. We're mountain people; we don't go into town much. I reckon we will now, though," he says, almost challenging me.

And then it starts to sink in. Perhaps my richness has caused me to become complacent. I haven't even been on the lookout at all for competition these past four years. Have I let my big swinging dick get the best of me? I shake this notion off, and quickly regain my composure.

"Where does the name Schläger come from?"

"It's German and Dutch, I'm told. Just like former president Martin Van Buren."

"*Really?* He took a shit in my outhouse as a kid."

"You don't say?" he says as he softens. "Hey, man, I think we got off on the wrong foot. Would you like to join us for lunch and our ritual bukkake session?"

Shit. I hesitate, trying to resist, but he has found my weakness. "Yes. Yes, I would."

As much as I hate what's going on right now, a man never turns down a bukkake session. It's just disrespectful. I begrudgingly follow the Schlägers as they head toward the tent. I'm definitely not in the right headspace you need to be in for an impromptu bukkake sesh. The biggest one smiles and pats me on the back.

"Guess we could have left our pants off, boys!" he says.

Everyone laughs as we walk into the huge tent. Mountains of gold nuggets rest on tables and makeshift scales. A huge pile of gold that has been ground down to dust is being divided by a couple brothers. One of them rolls up a dollar bill and snorts a monster fucking line of it. Next. Level. Shit. Holmes. He turns and hands me the rolled-up dollar and points to a huge rail.

"You want a toot?"

"No. I want *two*."

Feeling everyone's eyes on me, I pull out my own double-nostril, gold-encrusted customized snorter and pile-drive two lines at once, one up each nostril. A hush falls over the room, and the brothers nod at one another, impressed. Another topless blonde woman grabs my arm and whispers in my ear.

"This way, sir," she says seductively in a Dutch accent.

She leads me in another direction, where I see another smaller tent inside the tent I'm currently in. A tent inside of another tent = mind blown.

Inside the smaller tent, I see more Schläger brothers standing in a line with their pants off in front of yet another beautiful nude blonde chick kneeling on the floor. It's your standard line for an informal bukkake session, so I drop my pants and wait my turn along with everyone else. As I stand there, cock exposed, I realize the unfathomable has happened—I'm not even excited.

Thousands of years ago, Asians created bukkake sessions as a way to garner trust and assert fairness after sealing a business transaction. It showed peace and harmony. Right now, I feel as if I am sealing *my* business fate by standing in this line. Good thing that it's common law that another man is not permitted to look another man in the eye during the ceremony. If so, they would see my trepidation as my turn approaches.

"Are you nervous?" asks the beautiful blonde woman kneeling on the floor staring up at me.

"Yeah, I'm nervous . . . for *you*," I say, as I fake a laugh.

As I tug on my penis, it feels like I am holding a wet sock. Son of a bitch, *not here, not now*. This can't happen. I need to show that mentally I have not been shaken by what has transpired, and I need to do it in impressive fashion. So I have to dig deep. I pull out the mental shovel and go inside my mind grave, also known as the "go-to."

Way, *way* back in the depths of every man's mind, they have that one go-to night. The one night that was so magical that no matter what horrific sexual situation you've gotten yourself into, you can think of this night to finish the job. A man may go to this night a hundred times over the course of his life, depending on what his lifestyle is like. I have never gone there before, but I can't show weakness in front of these men.

So I close my eyes and go there, stroking with the precision of the Harvard crew team. My go-to is the night of May 21, 1839, when my dad had finally let me drive the wagon into town by myself for the first time to pick up two sacks of oats for our family. He handed me two loaded shotguns before I left and said, "Watch out for Indians; they've been robbing white people."

As I rode into town, I was stopped by a hollering group of them, faces painted. Up close, I realized they were all girls, and they were hot as fuck. Without saying a single word, they proceeded to rob me . . . of my *virginity*. They tied me down inside the back of my wagon and raped me for hours.

Right around dawn of the following morning as the sun was rising, they gave up. One of them proposed to me when she finished. Three others were weeping as they kissed and washed my feet, calling me Spirit Dick. The last one wiped her face paint off and told me she was white, which wasn't true. That's the kind of sexual power I held, even as a boy.

As I look down at the chick kneeling on the ground in front of me, I hit my stride. Just when I am about to unload a triple-roper, I grab my bloody SJSJ handkerchief from my pocket and squeeze it tightly, screaming out "Freedom!"

Shivering as if there is a chill in the air, I slowly release the hanky. By the time it hits the ground, my balls are backdrafting up into my body, and I ejac with a force that would baffle seismologists for years. The woman seems to be in shock as I take a moment to admire my masterpiece. Her body now resembles a Jackson Pollock painting. She blinks her eyes and nods in appreciation.

After I zip up, I nod at the next man, letting him know that I'm safely finished and he can begin. On the way out of the tiny tent, I run into the eldest Schläger. He smiles and extends his hand.

"Did you have a good time?" he asks.

"I'm not shaking your hand, dude. We were just touching our dicks."

"So? We're rich, it doesn't count."

"It only *doesn't* count if we just completed a business transaction."

"You're right. Let me buy your gold mine. Name your price."

"Fuck you. If I sell to you, you'll be able to control the town."

"We already control the town. Now we want *everything*."

"You control the town? That will be the fucking day. You might control this mountain, but definitely not the town. I'm still the candyman to all the toothless children!"

Forcing a laugh, I seal the top button on my jeans and reattach my sidearms. Although my confidence is shaken, I grab my dick like a man, never flinching. I stare him down with lifeless eyes, as if I have Down's syndrome.

"You know, I never did catch your first name," I calmly say.

"It's Sven."

"Seven?"

"No, *Sven*. No first *e*—it's Dutch. Why do you give a shit?"

"Well, you have to pay the engraver by the letter on your tombstone. If I were you, I'd have your brothers just ask for the numeral. It'll be cheaper."

I whistle for my steed and walk out without ever breaking eye contact or blinking. Sven screams, "This is just the beginning! We'll be everywhere soon!"

As I ride out, I think of how proud I am for pulling off that triple-roper in the bukkake sesh. But now what do I do about *not* being the richest man I know? I can't let a bunch of Dutch rednecks take me down. That's when it suddenly dawns on me—I need to buy up every fucking thing in town. I dig my heels hard into my steed and head straight to the deed office.

An enormous sense of urgency swells as I ride down Main Street, partially because a full string section is playing in the town square, begging for money. Street musicians are the worst. We get it, you're poor. Move on. I tie up my steed and walk inside the deed office, where I'm greeted by a long line of the filthiest sons of bitches you can imagine. Picture the people in line at a DMV and the entire front row of defendants at a DUI court combined. Yeah, let that wine breathe for a sec. Plus, showers don't really exist yet, so all these people stink like ten thousand Mexicans took a shit in their hands.

The deed office is a place where people of every walk of life are just trying to claim anything they can get their disgusting hands on. Think about it—Alaska doesn't even exist yet in the 1800s. It is just a cold place where you can fuck bears if you are into that. I could buy the entire state for eighty dollars.

After thirty seconds, I'm fed up with the line, so I pull out my gun and fire it into the ceiling six times. Everyone hits the floor, and I walk toward the front.

"I'm Saint James Street James, the richest man in town, and I'm skipping this line."

Nobody says shit to me as I walk to the first deed teller, an old man in his seventies with one foot in the grave. He stares at me through a monocle. His name is John Monopoly. This guy is a fucking asshole—even his own family hates him.*

"What can I do for you on this fine day?" he says as he peers at me over the counter.

"I'd like to buy every gold mine in town, please."

He pulls out a large, old map that looks like something Ponce de León used to jizz into on long voyages. You can actually hear it crack as he opens it. He slams it down on the counter in front of him, staring at it carefully.

---

* Years later his grandson created a board game named after him to make his name synonymous with families arguing over shitty deeds. That kid even named a property after me.

"Sorry, sir, but they're all bought up!" he says.

"By who?"

"The Schläger Brothers. They bought up every mine in town, except yours, of course. Next!"

"Hang on, you old bag of dicks, I want to buy some more shit."

"What do you have in mind?"

"How about some of the *other* mines?" I say in a lower register.

"I told you all the other gold mines are all bought up."

I lean across the counter and whisper quietly, "How about the silver or copper mines?"

"What's that you say? I can't hear you!"

"Do you have any silver or copper mines for sale?" I ask, slightly raising my voice.

"You say you want to buy silver or copper mines!"

Everyone in the entire deed office stops and stares. After a long pause, they begin laughing at me uncontrollably. A dirty-looking Mexican man starts pointing at me, turning to the line.

"Copper and silver? That's what us poor people buy!" he laughs.

I unholster my pistol and shoot him right in the heart. He hits the ground dead as shit. Everyone quickly averts their eyes from me as the dead man is dragged out. Mr. Monopoly leans across the counter and motions me toward him with his index finger.

"Mr. Street James, if you want my friendly advice, I'd start saving some of your money." An audible gasp can be heard from the patrons behind me.

"Did you just try to 'son' me by spewing out financial advice?" I ask.

Mr. Monopoly immediately tries to backtrack. "I . . . I didn't . . ."

"Too late."

I stand up from the desk, calmly pull out my gun, and blow this motherfucker away. To emphasize my point, I pull out my other gun, unleashing the entire cylinder into him after he is already dead.

I jump up onto the counter and yell, "Let's get one thing straight! Saint James Street James is still the richest motherfucker in this town, and for your troubles, here's some gold."

Digging into my pockets, I take out handfuls of gold chunks and throw them on the floor just to watch these grimy bastards dive on the ground to fight over them like the peasants they are. I smile to myself as I walk out. It's been a long fucking day, and I need a drink, maybe a prosty or two. I deserve it.

Chapter Five

THE WILD WEST WAS RAD, BECAUSE YOU COULD JUST KILL PEOPLE

Over the next six months, the Schläger brothers slowly integrate into society and spend their gold throughout town. I see these assholes every day. It is jolting looking at these rednecks riding down Main Street hollering weird incestuous innuendo toward one another.

"I'm gonna suck your dick!" one of them screams out.

"Not if I suck yours first!" another one laughs. "Just kidding, but not if it's dark, then you'll never know it was me!"

After a long day, I don't need to hear that shit, I just want a drink and ten sets of tits in my face. When I hop down from my steed, I see my favorite sleepy little whorehouse going off like electricity has just been invented. I walk in and see a midget dressed in only a tuxedo shirt and jacket, naked from the waist down, playing the piano like a tiny little Chopin. All the whores are topless, dancing on top of the tables.

Two of them are making out with each other on a makeshift stage that has been set up in the back of the saloon. The Schläger brothers are front and center throwing tiny chunks of gold onto the stage. They raise mason jars full of liquor and toast each other, laughing like animals. My blood begins to boil. Behind the bar, I see Manuel serving as many drinks as he can. I have to fight my way through the crowd to get to him.

"Manny, what the shit is happening in here?"

"The Schläger brothers came in this morning and have been giving out free liquor all day," he screams back over the madness.

"So what? I buy drinks for the entire place all the time."

"Yeah, but this new liquor is fucking crazy, man. Everyone is going banana-dick over it! People take a shot of it and lose their mind!"

"What is it?"

Manuel grabs a bottle from behind the bar and hands it to me. The label reads "Goldschläger." I feel like he has just handed me the first breast implant. I've never seen anything like it.

"It's some crazy hybrid liquor from Europe and West Virginia. It's got real chunks of gold in it, man! How fucking crazy is that? Here, have a shot. Everything is on the house today, courtesy of the Schlägers."

Manuel pours me a shot and slides it down the bar. He holds up his own shot and we "air cheers," drinking it together. Goddamn it, this shit is smooth. Manuel looks at me, and his eyes start rolling into the back of his head. I'm confused, until I see a woman pop up and wipe the side of her mouth. He was getting blown the whole time we were talking. Jesus, man, *that guy never gets blown, either.* People really are going bug-fuck over this shit. He pours another shot and slings it to me.

"This is the greatest day of my life!" Manuel screams. "It's like people forgot that I'm an Indian and they're treating me like a real person!"

He rips his leather vest off and throws it out into the crowd. Staring into the clear liquor, I see the gold flakes floating around in a trancelike motion, as if they are dancing along with the music from the piano. Clear liquor doesn't exist in these parts, let alone liquor with chunks of gold in it. All I can think about is how rich the Schläger brothers keep getting. They've almost taken over the entire town in just a little over half a year, and now they're *so* rich that they will make other people shit gold after drinking their liquor.

Does this mean poor people will be digging into their own shit so they can turn a profit? Will this change the balance of power between the classes? Are people going to be holding guns to each other's heads and asking them to shit their pants so they can get a score? Why am I thinking about this? I snap out of it, take the shot, and slam it on the table. A man's hand slaps me on the shoulder from behind.

"That drink is the shit, ain't it?"

I quick-draw and fire a shot into his stomach, then re-holster without even turning around. The entire bar grinds to a halt and stares at me. Even the half-nude midget pianist stops playing and runs out of the bar. I glance down at the man I just shot, recognizing his face. It's one of the Schläger brothers from the bukkake line. He looks up at me in disbelief as he coughs up blood.

"Why did you do that?" he asks.

"No one asks me to drink *and* shit, you hear me?"

"I said this drink *is* the shit. Now I'm dead."

He closes his eyes and dies on the floor. The other Schläger brothers get up from their chairs and rush me, forming a half-circle. I do my best to keep my back pressed against the bar, so they can't surround me. The half-nude midget runs back in and quickly grabs his bowler hat from on top of the piano, before running back out. Where the fuck is he going that he needs his hat? Sven, the beefy Schläger brother from earlier, steps out in front of the half-circle.

"You killed my brother."

"You got fifteen more."

"You think I'm going to let you drink my free liquor, kill one of my brothers, and I'm just going to be cool with it?"

"If you want to go against the hand of God, may peace be with you," I say, as I point to my gun.

Manuel pipes up in the background, "Don't do it! Saint James Street James is the fastest gun I've ever seen. He'll kill all of you."

"Is that so?" Sven says.

"He's full of shit, Sven!" one of the youngest brothers screams. Another brother suddenly gets brave and pulls out his pistol. Before he can even raise it past his belt line, I shoot him three times in the head, dropping him to the floor like a wet turd from a man on stilts. The Schlägers howl in rage.

"That's two of my brothers! You're a goddamn dead man, Saint James," Sven seethes.

"I'd hate to kill another one; I don't think you can count that high."

As Sven begins to do a silent count staring at his fingers, I shoot the two bottles of Goldschläger that Manuel is holding, and the contents explode all over the floor. Every whore in the joint hits the ground and tries to scoop up the gold flakes before they disappear beneath the floorboards. Amidst the frenzy, I tip my hat to Sven and walk out.

Once outside, I see my Chinaman running toward me. He's out of breath and thirsty as shit, per usual. He's trying to speak but doesn't have enough saliva to physically get the words out. I pull out a canteen from my saddlebag and give it to my horse to drink.

"Spit it out, man, I don't have all fucking day."

He licks his lips and finally musters up the words, "Boss . . . no more gold."

"What did you say? Because it sounded like you said *'no more gold'*!"

He nods his head yes and then passes out from dehydration. I examine his hands and notice that he has all ten fingers. It's definitely *my* Asian. I throw his unconscious body up on the back of my steed, and we ride out toward my gold mine.

It's a ten-mile ride, which is even longer when you have a foul-smelling half-dead Chinaman bouncing back and forth against you from behind. When we finally reach the mine, I pull another canteen out of my saddlebag and pour a small amount of water on my Chinaman's lips. He licks it softly and stirs to life, bowing appreciatively toward me.

"Thank you, boss, thank you."

"No problem," I say as I then proceed to dump the rest of the canteen all over my face, neck, and hands to wash off the trip. "Take me inside the mine."

We fire up two lanterns and walk into the filthy mine. Soon I am further inside than I've ever been. I shine my lantern toward the walls, and I'm in awe of what I see. From ceiling to floor are elaborate drawings of people hardcore fucking. There are also drawings of a guy getting killed over and over again in different, horrendous ways. The closer I study them, it appears to be the same guy who is getting killed, and the guy in the drawings resembles *me*. I mean, they look *exactly* like me.

"How old do you think these drawings are?"

"Probably a few hours ago? I started to think I was going to die of thirst in this mine."

"Is this me, the guy who keeps getting killed over and over?"

The Chinaman sheepishly looks away. "Nope. Different guy. Old boss. You guys were the same height, that's all."

The further we go, all I see are rocks, without a speck of gold to be found. The Chinaman picks up a hammer and pick, banging against a wall of solid rock. After a few hits, chunks of rock fall from the wall to the ground. I pick them up and examine them with my lantern. Nothing. Panic and desperation set in, and I sit down inside the mine. For a brief second, I wonder if I can just paint the rocks yellow and pass them off—maybe no one will know. My Chinaman slinks down next to me.

"What are we going to do, boss?"

"Well, I have a ton of gold that you've dug up for me over the last couple years. I suppose I can live off that. You?"

"Not sure. You've only paid me one cent a day the entire time I've been working for you, which has only afforded me rice and water for my family. Most days, I usually give my ration of water to my children, and I go thirsty."

"Have you been thirsty? I hadn't noticed. Sorry about that. Here you go." I pull yet another canteen out of my jacket and hand it to him.

He smiles, genuinely touched. "Thank you."

"No problem. Good luck with everything."

When I pat him on the shoulder and walk out, I don't even have to turn back around to know that he appreciated the old "empty canteen trick." As I finally make my way out, I ride off into the forest in silence. Usually I sing Negro spirituals aloud when I ride home from work, but today my sadness has overtaken me.

Making my way out of the trees, I can see my property from the top of the hill. I hear a loud scream that I would recognize anywhere echo from the low land. It's Louretta. In a panic, I ride hard down the hill toward the house. A scream like that can only mean one thing . . . someone is dead.

As I get closer, I see my kids outside crying next to her. She's lying on the ground screaming and pointing to the top of the barn, where I see what appears to be a large, gold statue swinging from a noose. I run toward her, confused.

"What the hell is going on? Why are you crying?"

"I can't—it's just—it's Totally Fucking Mexico out there!" she wails.

"Shit got *that* wild?"

"No, it's our third-youngest son, Totally Fucking Mexico. He's dead."

"Sorry, I always forget we named him on vacation. Where's his body?"

She points up to the golden statue and screams, "That's him right there! They dipped him in a pot of melted gold!"

I look up at Totally Fucking Mexico hanging there, frozen in solid gold. The rage inside me begins to boil. I'm barely able to get out the words, "Who did this?"

"I don't know who they were! They grabbed me when I was inside cooking dinner, but I didn't recognize them. All of them had gold teeth."

"Listen to me, Lou. I want you to know that I will find the motherfuckers who did this, and they will pay with their own lives."

My wife stares daggers at me as she sobs uncontrollably, knowing full well I already know who killed him. I hold her in my arms as I look down at my children. All of them are crying except for Daniel, my eldest, who has a look of anger in his eyes like he wants to kill. It's the same look I've had my whole life.

"Lou, put the kids in their rooms. I want to talk to Daniel alone."

"All right," she says as she wipes away her tears and takes the other kids upstairs.

"What happened here today, boy?" I ask Daniel.

"Mom was cooking dinner while me and the boys were playing hide and never come back. All of the sudden, this group of rowdy redneck men came riding out of the woods and scooped up Totally

Fucking Mexico. They said something about you killing their brothers and that this was an eye for an eye. One of the brothers was riding with a wagon towing a cauldron. They put a bunch of gold in it, built a fire, waited for it to melt, then threw him in. And they made Mom watch."

"Our neighbor, Mr. Paulson, didn't help out?

"Nope."

"That motherfucker. I'll deal with him later. Women are off-limits obviously, but I killed two of theirs—why didn't they try and kill two of you?"

"I told you, we were hiding . . . and *never* coming back."

"Why weren't you coming back?"

"Because we hate you." He slowly pulls a Buck knife from behind his back that has blood dripping off of it.

"Good, you're supposed to hate your father. Why is there blood on your knife?"

"They rode out in the forest past me after they hung Totally Fucking Mexico. I jumped out from behind a tree and got one in the leg. He fell off his horse, but I don't think they noticed."

"Is he still out there?"

"I think so. He was bleeding real good."

"All right, I'm proud of you. Go grab the ladder and cut down your brother. I'll see if that man is still out there."

When he runs off, I well up with fatherly pride. I don't know if it's possible for a male's balls to drop around eight years old, but I'll be goddamned if that little motherfucker's didn't hit the dirt in that moment. He's growing up to be a badass right before my very eyes.

Looking down, I spot a trail of blood on the ground leading into the woods. As I follow it to the tree line, I can hear a male grunting. It's either a man dying, or someone in the end stages of a sweet j-off sesh. Up ahead in the trail, I see a half-drunk bottle of Goldschläger with a bloody handprint on it. I stop and pick it up, and the grunting gets louder.

Ahead in the distance, I spot one of the fat little Schläger brothers propped up against a tree, tying a knot around a knife wound in his leg with a ripped-off shirtsleeve. I casually stroll over to him and clear my throat loudly.

"Did your hymen break?" I ask.

The tubby little haunted troll goes to grab his gun, but I quick-draw mine and put a bullet through his hand. His gun flies ten feet backward and he screams in anguish. His face turns pale as I laugh and take a long pull of Goldschläger.

"You want some? Me, I'm not a fan of this shit. There's just too much fucking 'gay' in it. You can have it."

I pour out all of the contents of the bottle into his open wound. He screams and clutches his leg like a beaten woman. The rest is kind of hazy. I don't know what proof that Goldschläger is, but that shit has been sneaking up on me all day. The last thing I remember is him begging for his life, crying, and saying he'll do anything I want, along with the requisite "please don't kill me" bullshit. Obviously I execute him using every bullet inside my gun, probably starting with non-vital organs first, ending his life really slowly so he feels every single shot fired. The one thing I'm not positive about is if I pissed on his dead body or not afterward.*

With the sun starting to set behind me, I button my pants and walk out of the forest. Through the kitchen window I can see my wife and kids sitting at the dinner table, preparing to eat. Louretta is valiantly trying to hold it together as tears stream down her face. I take off my hat when I walk in and join them at the table. She grabs the hands of our boys sitting on both sides of her and bows her head.

"Please join hands in a moment of silence for Totally Fucking Mexico," she says softly.

Just as we bow our heads, we hear the rope being cut and a loud *gong* sound outside from the statue hitting the ground.

"I cut him down, Dad!" Daniel screams out.

Louretta loses it and bursts into hysterics. She takes her napkin off her lap and throws it on the table, excusing herself. The rest of us sit in silence as we pick at our meal. I consider saying something to her about burning the veal as she is leaving but think better of it at the last second. I'll tell her tomorrow. Daniel walks in and sits across from me at the table.

"Dad, did you K-I-L-L that guy in the forest?"

"Yeah, and I fucking U-R-I-N-A-T-E-D on him too."

He stares at me, confused, as do the rest of my children. If he's going to spell shit out like he's a big man, he better know all the

---

* I'm not kidding. I used to do shit like that, just so people had a really fucked-up mental experience before they left this earth. Wait, now I remember. Of course I fucking pissed on him. He killed my son.

big-boy words. I try to eat my shitty food, but I can't stop thinking about all the different ways that I'm going to fuck up my neighbor, Mr. Paulson, when he gets home.

I know he works late, because each of us only has one neighbor, and you know everything about them. You go to church with them on Sundays, cook each other pies, biscuits, casseroles, all that bullshit. More important, you look after them and make sure they are safe. As a man, you know to look out for your neighbor's wife and kids if they are in trouble. Guy-code shit.

Instead, my cocksucking neighbor Ron Paulson did nothing, and for that, he will feel my fucking wrath. I'd ride down to his office now, but it's best if I catch him right when he walks into his house, so I can beat him in front of his wife. This will ensure a mental scar that will stay with him forever and make him feel weaker in her presence every time they're together the rest of their lives. I'm going to enjoy every fucking second of it too. I know that may sound sick, but you don't just sit there with your hands on your dick while your neighbor's kid is getting dipped in hot gold. My four-year-old, whose name I'm blanking on, looks up at me deep in thought.

"Dad, should I bring some veal and cabbage out to Totally Fucking Mexico?" he asks.

All my boys look up at me for an answer. For the first time ever, I have to be a real father. My voice cracks, and I'm barely able to muster up the words, "He's not very hungry right now, and he wants me to have it."

I take his plate and scrape his meal onto mine before I get up. On the way out, I lean down and whisper into Daniel's ear, "You're the oldest, so I want you to keep an eye on your brothers tonight. I gotta go ball your mom. She's probably grieving, so don't disturb us unless it's an emergency."

Daniel nods silently as I head into the bedroom with my double plate of veal and cabbage. I'm fucking starving, but I know I'm not going to get to eat anytime soon. As I close the bedroom door behind me, a large perfume bottle whizzes by my head and smashes against the top of the door frame. Louretta is crying hysterically, looking for something else to throw. She sees my prized banjo hung on the wall and grabs it by the neck, raising it above her head.

"I hate you!" she screams.

"Don't you fucking dare throw it! That's my *favorite* banjo!"

"You did this! You're the reason he died, asshole!"

I quickly put my dinner plate down on the bed and sprint over to her, grabbing her arms before she can throw the banjo at me. We struggle, then I squeeze a pressure point under her armpit and she slowly releases it, crumpling to the floor, sobbing. I take the banjo and carefully hang it back on the wall, where it belongs.

"You care more about that goddamn banjo than you do your own family!" she wails.

She gets up and starts punching my chest, yelling, "You killed him! You killed my third-youngest baby boy! He was my favorite!"

I grab her and pull her tightly into my flexed pecs. "I loved him too! That kid was worth his weight in—"

Shit. I knew it the second it came out of my mouth. Louretta tries to shove me away from her, but it's like trying to push a mountain up *another* mountain. She slaps me hard across the face, and I slap her right back. She then spits at me, which I catch with my hand, jamming it down my pants, using it to gently stroke my cock to get it hard. I lift her up against the nightstand while she tries to squirm away.

"What are you doing?" she shouts.

"Giving you that child that was just taken from you. Time to get pregnant."

I put my finger on her mouth, shushing her, because I'm pretty sure she's going to try and say something. This isn't a time for words; it's a time for lovemaking. The type of lovemaking I participate in when a child dies is different. It's furious and unrestrained. It's the type of love where you use quick, short thrusts while pulling the back of each other's hair with a firm grip. Both parties exert a lot of raw emotions, and the sex is intense. You also never break eye contact, because in a fucked-up way, you're glad you're still alive, and happy you're not the one who's frozen in gold. Quietly, I ask her if she wants to climax with me. She nods as I scream out into the night, "Your death will not go unavenged, *Mejico!*"

We climax hard together—hers lasting longer than mine, obviously. She falls to the ground on top of me and begins sobbing lightly. I wipe her tears away and tuck her hair back behind her ears, because it's in my face and I can't see anything.

"You're definitely pregnant after that."

She exhales deeply and says, "I'm sure of it."

I scoop her up off the floor and lay her on the bed next to my plate of food. "Don't eat that," I say as I head over to the wall and grab my banjo.

She nods knowingly and positions herself against the headboard, holding my dinner plate. I nestle myself between her thighs and begin to play a tune for her as she feeds me my dinner. She sways her head slowly to the rhythm and continues to feed me as I pluck my 'jo seductively.

"What happened out there today, Saint James?"

"I kilt summon ta dahay."

"What? I can't understand you, your mouth is full of food."

I swallow and look off into the distance. "I killed some men today. Also, we might be out of gold."

"What do you mean we might be out of gold?"

"The mine is empty. I sent my Chinaman home. We've got enough here to live off of for the rest of our lives anyway."

"Actually, we don't. Those men took all of our gold out of the barn and put it in that cauldron to melt and throw Totally Fucking Mexico into."

I stop playing my banjo. "What? They covered Totally Fucking Mexico *in my own gold*?"

"Yes. All of it."

"And Mr. Paulson did nothing to stop that either?"

She shakes her head no. "Maybe it's not a bad thing, us losing all our gold. You've become a different person since you struck it rich. I miss the old you. We were so much happier when we were simple farmers working eighteen hours a day all seven days a week just to live."

She knows I hate when she talks about me being poor, but she goes there anyway. I stand up and carefully place my banjo back on the wall, before putting my jeans on. "Maybe you were. You pretty much just hung out and did the same shit you were doing now, cooking and cleaning, tending to the kids and whatnot. I was out there busting my balls wide open every day just so we could eat shit made out of cornmeal."

I put my boots on, throw on a shirt, and holster up as I walk out.

"Where are you going, Saint James?"

"To handle shit like a boss. First stop, Mr. Paulson's. That fuck should be home by now."

On my way out, I see Daniel sharpening his knife on the front porch. He looks up at me as I pass him. "Are you going to kill the rest of those men, Pa?"

"No, son. When you kill someone, or multiple people in the same family like I did, the rule of thumb is you give them a week to grieve before you kill another relative. That's why I'm going to give Mr. Paulson a workout."

"Can I come with you?"

"Sorry, but you're too young to see something like this go down. This is some old-school shit that will fuck a man up on the inside."

Daniel smiles at me as I hop on my steed and head off into the night. This is a revenge ride, so there's really no need to explain in great detail how my pecs are flexing at a max level as I glide on my horse alongside the river, down to Mr. Paulson's house. I've got other shit on my mind. I do, however, manage to take a glance at my reflection in the water and see my triceps ripple as I hold the reins. They're as perfect as you can imagine.

Chapter Six

TIME TO TAKE A SHIT IN MY OWN HANDS. I THINK THAT SENTENCE IS WRONG.

Riding up to Mr. Paulson's house, I laugh to myself at the size of it. Bullshit realtors would call it "modest," but let's call a spade a spade here: the fucking thing looks like elves or cobblers live in it. As I'm tying up my steed, I notice that even his horse is shittier than mine. My steed resembles a goddamn racehorse, his looks like it has been giving ghost tours to carriages full of tourists downtown for thirty years. I reach down and move the eating trough and put it in front of my steed.

"You can fuck that other horse when you're done eating if you want to. I left enough slack in those reins," I whisper.

He winks at me as I knock on the door. A woman in her early thirties, Sheila Paulson, answers and is immediately taken aback by my presence. She quickly tries to fuss with her hair to pretty herself up, but let me tell you, she's giving you a five back when you hand her a ten. Trying to fix her hair at the last second isn't going to make her a six.

"Why, Saint James, Ron didn't tell me you were coming over."

"I know. You would have made yourself look prettier. Did Ron tell you anything about what happened today up at my place?"

"No. I heard some screaming, but Ron told me to hide in the bedroom and put a pillow over my face. He said we shouldn't get involved."

"Did he now? Where is Ron?"

As soon as the question leaves my lips, Ron appears through the backdoor of the house with a newspaper under his arm, holding a lit lantern. He's a taller, gimpy, balding man in his forties who owns the town printing press. What you're picturing in your head right now *is exactly what he looks like.* His face freezes in fear at the sight of me standing in his living room.

"Hey, Ron, how was your day?"

"It, it, it was good, you know? I was just reading over tomorrow's newspaper before it goes to print in the morning."

"Reading it over a nice hearty deuce I see."

"Well, no—I was just out back, reading it by lantern."

"May I see it?"

"Sure," he says, somewhat surprised.

He hands me the paper, and I read over it quickly, shaking my head in mock disappointment. I then hold it up for him to see the entire front page, tilting it from side to side.

"It's strange. I don't see a headline in here that says, 'Four-Year-Old Boy Killed from Being Dipped into Scalding Hot Gold While Neighbor Watches and Does Nothing.'"

"Probably because that would be a run-on sentence. You can't join two independent clauses . . ." he cuts himself off and quickly looks away. "I don't have any idea what you're talking about," he finishes.

"You don't? That's odd. Because your wife said you made her hide in the bedroom and put a pillow over her face while the screaming was going on up at my house today."

"That screaming could have been for anything, Saint James. You and your wife have sex a lot."

"Normally that excuse would fly, because it's true, but did you not hear a little boy's voice crying out as well? You know I never fuck directly in front of my children. If you had any children of your own, you would understand."

"We've been trying, Saint James, but Sheila just can't."

"She can't . . . or *you* can't?"

"Saint James, that's not fair."

"It's hot in here. You mind if I take off my shirt, Ron?"

"No, please don't—"

It's too late. I've already taken off my shirt and placed it on his coatrack. Ron nervously shakes his head as Sheila licks her lips slightly. I'm not going to lie—I may have thrown on a half-inch of butter on the ride over just to accentuate my physique. Deliberately, I begin to take off my belt, loop by loop. As the belt slithers through each rung, Ron is visibly shaking like a man with Parkinson's holding a set of wind chimes.

Once I've successfully pulled my belt all the way through, I snap it in the air. I crack my neck back and forth, before slowly walking over to Ron. Out of my peripheral vision, I spot a bowl of water to wash up in, and I dip my belt into it. Ron puts his hands up in front of his face.

"Saint James, please, sir!"

"Aw, look at you. You're putting your hands up to protect yourself. I wish someone would have protected my little boy today *before he was melted into hot fucking gold*!"

Ron flinches and covers his head as I unleash my belt right across the fat part of his back. He buckles to the floor and lets out a high-pitched, preteen white girl scream. I bet Daniel is on the front porch back home smiling, listening to this little pigshit cry. Ron balls himself up into the fetal position on the ground, preparing for the worst, which is coming.

I rise up again and again, continuing to beat him with my wet belt. In my blind rage, I look over and see Sheila hiding behind a door, peeking out at me. I notice her smirking through clenched teeth. Each time I beat Ron, she seems more into it, as if she's rooting for me. She bites her lip seductively.

"You enjoy watching me humiliate him like this?"

"Yes," she says softly.

Ron looks at her with disdain, but she ignores him and starts to undo her dress with a zeal she probably hasn't experienced since she was nineteen. Her dress hits the floor, and Sheila shows no shame. Most women her age would try and cover up, but she doesn't even flinch. She may be a five on the outside, but goddamn if she hasn't been hiding a seven body underneath her colonial dress all these years.

"I want you to fuck me like I deserve it," she says.

"No. I'm going to fuck you like *Ron* deserves it."

Ron begs through muffled tears, "Please, I beg you, I can't take this."

He didn't have a hard time hearing my son beg for his life, so me fucking his wife in front of him on the family kitchen table that they eat from every night is only fair. I take Ron's arms and legs and methodically hog-tie this fat fucker on the floor with my belt. After I'm satisfied that he can't move, I push him over so he's on his side, facing up at the table.

Taking two long Bigfoot strides over to Sheila, I lift her up and insert myself into her at the same time. We crash against the kitchen wall and make out like two Mexican teenagers underneath a picnic table at a *quinceañera*. Pots and pans hanging from above crash to the floor. Without looking down, I kick them at Ron while I grab Sheila's surprisingly firm ass as I walk-fuck her over to the table.

With my free arm, I clear off a delicious dinner of sautéed carrots and a skirt steak that she has made for Ron. The plates shatter right in front of his face as well. His sobbing isn't enough for me; it's time for the real emotional scarring. I begin to fuck Sheila like Ron never could in a million goddamn years. With her back on the table, I lift her legs up above my shoulders.

For Ron's wife, because I respect her, I go with the jackhammer because I want to maintain a controlled amount of penetration, with rhythmic timing. I also want Ron to know that this move is part of my regular arsenal and that I can maintain it for long periods of time, something he could never do. Again, I cannot stress how important my sexual precision is in moments like these. It adds years of destruction to someone's conscience.

With a decent sweat worked up, I walk over to the wood-burning oven, still full-bone, and open the door so it gets even hotter in here. We're now licking each other's sweat and biting one another. Sheila asks me to choke her, and of course I oblige. Just as she can't take it anymore, I tell her I'm going to climax *with* her. Climaxing with someone's wife in front of them is the final nail in the coffin. I look over to Ron, who is sweating profusely and crying. He just wants this to end, but I won't let it quite yet. I snap my fingers to get his full attention.

"I want you to listen to me, Ron, as I climax. I want you to look me in the eyes. Do you understand?"

Through his crying, he weakly says "Okay." With eye contact established, I pick up the pace of my thrusts and apply more pressure to Sheila's throat. She starts moaning like she's from a foreign country. As I climax, I hear my steed climax outside as well, which makes me happy to know that my horse fucked Ron's horse too. With our eyes still fixated on one another's, I squint intensely and whisper to Ron, "I now live inside your mind forever."

Mentally and physically broken, he closes his eyes and he blacks out from the heat. I rise up off Sheila and thank her, but she has no words. She instead takes my hand and begins blessing herself sign-of-the-cross style, before I unwrap my belt from around Ron's arms and legs. His limbs hit the floor and he gingerly rolls over. Standing over him, I slap his face with my hand until his eyes open.

"I'll see you at the funeral this weekend. Sheila, its potluck, so if you could bring some potato salad, that would be amazing."

"Of course. See you then. Tell Louretta she's in our thoughts and prayers."

"I will."

I throw on my clothes and walk out the front door just in time to see my horse dismount Ron's horse. We both nod at each other for a job well done. As I'm pulling away, Sheila waves at me from the front porch. With the revenge factor taken care of with Ron, my mind shifts to my gold problem, and killing the rest of the Schläger brothers.

Per usual, I stop by the river outside my house to wash off my dick and balls. I only wish my dead son was able to be downriver so he could taste this. I dunk my entire body underwater and sit at the bottom of the river. A bright orb of light shines in front of my face in the water. I wipe my eyes and refocus, finally making out the image. It's Totally Fucking Mexico! He's staring straight at me, almost looking through me. In a *Tree of Life* whisper I hear him say the words, "I forgive you, Father . . . I *can* taste this water."

"Fuck. Yeah. That makes me happy."

His ghost then high-fives me before vanishing. I smile, at peace with myself and the life decisions I've made. I knew he'd understand. Realizing I've been underwater for almost eight minutes, I rise to the surface, gasping for air. I see the moon shining down on his dead, gold statue out in the yard, so I throw up an index finger in the air out of respect, like when Kobe left the court after dropping eighty-one on the Raptors.

Walking out of the river, I air-dry up to the house, where I see Daniel waiting for me on the front porch. He nods at me with a knowing smirk. To answer your question, no, I'm not uncomfortable being buck naked in front of my sons, either. I want them to know what they will look like in adulthood. It's a lot better than what any of their bullshit female teachers could teach them about puberty and becoming a man. This is the real shit, hanging brains right in his face. Daniel knows this and respects it.

"I know what you did out at Ron's farm, Dad."

"You do?"

He nods his head, "Yeah. I just want you to know . . . I shut the windows so Mom wouldn't hear."

"Thank you. That's what a real man does. I'm proud of you."

My dong grazes against his head as I lean in and hug him. Slightly embarrassed, I take a step back, realizing this is the first time I've ever hugged him. I take a seat next to him on the porch and grab a small tobacco tin that rests on the step. Shaking the remaining water off my hands, I pull out a couple rolling papers and hand-roll us two cigarettes just like my dad did for me around eight years old. He strikes a match off the porch and lights our smokes.

With his first inhale, he coughs a little, and I laugh at him and call him a bitch. It's one of those magical moments in life where you're able to sit down buck naked on the porch with your son after you've just fucked your neighbor's wife and share a smoke.

"Look at you trying to puff tough! I love it," I say to him.

"Are these things healthy for me?" Daniel asks, as he looks at the cigarette.

"A lot healthier than that bullshit milk your mom gives you. When's the last time you were at the doctor's office and he *wasn't* smoking?"

"Never."

"*Exactly.* Now, when's the last time you rolled into the doctor's and he was relaxing, drinking a warm glass of milk? *Never.* That was knowledge I just gave you."

"I guess you're right. What are you going to do about the Schlägers, Dad? Kill everyone in sight and take their gold?"

"I have to assess the situation and see how many there are. I don't want any more of you guys getting offed. I'm a fucking amazing human being, but I'm only one man. But yes, more than likely I'll start killing everyone real soon."

"If you need any help or a human shield or anything, I'm in."

"I don't think that will ever be necessary, but it's nice to know you'd do something like that for me."

"I'm tough, Dad. I will prove myself to you."

"You already have. I saw that Schläger you took out in the woods. Nice fucking work. See you tomorrow, cowboy."

I stand up and take one last drag off my cigarette before flicking it off into the yard. With the calmness of a rapist, I ease up the stairs of the house and sneak into bed with Louretta. I can still hear her sobbing as she stares out the window at the golden statue of our dead son in the yard.

"I'm going into town in the morning to make funeral arrangements. Do you want to come with me?" I ask.

"No. I can't bear to see those tiny coffins."

"Have you thought about cremation? We sure could use the gold right about now."

"Don't you fucking dare! Our son deserves a proper burial!"

"Okay, we'll table that convo for the night."

The following morning we eat our breakfast in silence, and for the first time in forever, it does not consist of gold. Have you ever eaten eggs or pancakes without gold on them? Let me tell you, it sucks. This is my first taste of poverty in a few years, and I am not fucking happy about it. I throw down my fork and head out, stopping only to rub the golden statue of my dead son for good luck.

Riding through the town street, I notice more people staring at me than usual. I look down to see if I have forgotten to place my cock inside my jeans, which happens more often than you think. This time we're all clear. Upon closer examination, I see everyone holding the morning newspaper. The headline reads, "Four-Year-Old Boy Killed from Being Dipped into Scalding Hot Gold," and the article is by Ron Paulson. See what deep-dicking someone's wife will get you? Respect. Men tip their hats toward me in silence as I pull up in front of Curly's Funeral Parlor.

When I walk inside, I'm immediately greeted by the owner, Curly, a burly sixty-five-year-old man who sports a large, gray handlebar mustache. His name is ironic, because he doesn't have a single hair on his head. This son of a bitch is also way too fucking chipper about owning a funeral parlor.

"How are you today, sir?" he asks with pep.

"Well, I'm at a goddamn funeral parlor. You?"

"Are you looking for something for you, or someone else?"

"No, it's not for me. I'm probably going to live forever. My four-year-old son passed away."

Curly shoots a look over to a newspaper laid out next to the register. He nods and looks down, wringing his hands nervously.

"Yeah, I'm real sorry to hear about that. I read about it in the paper this morning. We have some nice coffins along the wall over here."

I point to a small-sized one in the corner. "How much for that one?"

"One hundred dollars. That's an excellent choice for your child."

"Oh, that one isn't for my child. That one is in case my dick and balls get detached or just fall off my body from too much usage. I want my package to have a proper burial as well."

"Um, okay."

"No, my boy is going to need an adult-sized coffin. The gold has obviously added a lot of extra height and width to him."

"I understand. The adult ones are fifty dollars more."

I go to pull some gold from my pockets, when it suddenly dawns on me that I don't have any more. Nothing. Not even a little nugget hiding in my boot. Shit, I totally forgot that I threw the rest of it on the ground at the deed office. Panic sets in as my eyes dart around the room.

"I'm sorry, I don't have any gold on me right now; it's all on my son. Wow, I feel really embarrassed. This is like being bald and having a name like Curly, am I right?"

Curly laughs loudly and wipes his bald head with a handkerchief, trying to make me laugh. It's totally fake and canned. Following up that gem, he does a shitty little dance like he's a tiny monkey, which is also awkward and forced. As I'm watching this charade unfold, that's when two sacked plums smack me square in the chin: Holy shit, this is what polite people do to the poor to make them feel comfortable. This is the kind of shit that *used* to happen to me before I was rich.

My heart starts racing, and I blurt out, "I'll be back, sir. Just let me go back home and get some more gold. I definitely have a lot more of it. Gold, that is. Stacks of it. I'm just grieving. I'm going to grab a drink and get my mind right."

Curly takes a silver dollar out of his pocket and flips it to me. "Here. The first one is on me. I can't imagine what you're going through right now."

I snatch the coin out of the air and stare at it, lost in thought. Not only did someone try to cheer me up for being poor, but now he's giving *me* money. That's my thing; I throw money at people. Usually it's followed by laughter and the phrase "Here you go, broke dick" or "Thanks, whore." Now this bald son of a bitch is treating me like a shoeshine boy. I debate throwing the coin back in his face and then pissing my surname all over the coffins, but the sad truth is, I can't because I really want a fucking drink. Feeling completely out of my element, I catch myself bowing to him like a grateful butler, before turning and quickly leaving.

As I walk down Main Street, the townspeople's looks toward me seem more prevalent. Instead of thinking that everyone is looking at me for having the dead child dipped in gold, I begin to wonder if they pity me because I'm poor. Paranoia has set in, and I pull my hat down over my eyes as I walk toward the saloon, trying not to make eye contact with anyone.

Luckily, it's so early in the morning that there are not many patrons inside, and I'm able to take a seat at the bar alone. I could really use a good whore sesh right now, but I'll be goddamned if I'm going to end up as one of those poor bastards who's getting an HJ underneath a table out in the open for a quarter. Manuel comes over and greets me warmly. I notice an open newspaper on the bar, and I know what's coming.

"Sorry about your son, Saint James."

"It's fine. I have six more and probably one on the way after last night. Just get me a shot of whiskey."

He grabs a bottle under the bar and pours me a shot. Without looking at him, I take the silver dollar out and slide it across the bar. From behind me, a hand slams down on top of the coin. I immediately grab my gun and turn to see the eldest Schläger brother, Sven, standing over me with a shit-eating grin.* He looks down at the silver dollar and laughs.

"Well, the famous Saint James Street James is paying in *silver*? Ain't that a sight? Something happen to all your gold?"

"Gold is overrated these days. People act like they're *made out of it*."

Knowing I would I run into the Schlägers, I came prepared. I pull out a small glass jar that I tucked inside my boot and slam it on

---

* I'm not kidding, there is actual human shit in his teeth. People eat their own shit for fun in West Virginia, which is where that phrase originated.

top of the bar. A set of two testicles wobble around inside the jar. Sven looks at me curiously.

"What the fuck are those?"

"Those are your brother's nuts. I'd ask him if he wants them back, but he's dead."

Sven turns around toward a table in the back and starts counting his brothers on his fingers. He seems confused. Finally he just yells out, "Hey, did we lose another brother?"

All of his brothers start counting one another. It's a shit show. By my estimate, there are somehow seventeen Schlägers. The brothers have almost doubled from yesterday.

"Jesus, man, how many brothers do you have?"

"As fast as our sisters can make 'em."

"Is that supposed to be menacing? Because it sounds fucking disgusting!"

"Disgusting for *you*. We don't die, we multiply. That's what West Virginia does all up in your butthole."

I quick-draw my gun and put it under his chin. "There has never been a man up in my butthole. Understand?"

All at once I can hear the sounds of guns being drawn. I turn slowly and see a wide variety of different guns pointed at me: pistols, shotguns, even a few muskets. One of the brothers is holding what appears to be a sharpened tree branch. Manuel pulls out a shotgun from underneath the bar and fires it into the ceiling.

"Hey, boys, I don't want any more blood spilled in my bar."

I nod and put my gun away, as do the Schlägers. The one guy with the sharpened tree branch throws it on the ground.

"Out of respect for you and your beautiful whorehouse estab-lishment, I'll go, Manny," I say as I take the shot of whiskey and slam the glass down on the bar. On the way out, I eye-fuck the shit out of Sven.

"I'll see you soon," I say, holding up seven fingers in his face.

"Do you want us to come to your son's funeral?"

"That's sweet, but you guys would probably be disappointed. My wife isn't serving shit for food afterward."

"I was thinking we could just bring fourteen carrots," he says.

Sven and his brothers laugh like it's the funniest thing they've ever heard. I stop at the double doors, briefly thinking about turning and killing him right then and there. Better judgment gets the best of me, and I keep walking toward my steed.

The ride home feels like an acid trip. All I can see in front of me is Sven's shit-eating grin and Curly's look of surprise when I reached into my empty pockets, unable to pay for my kid's funeral. My world is crumbling. I don't want to go back to being a farmer, or a guy who has to get HJs out in the middle of the bar in front of everyone.

The glow of the sun from my kid's dead, golden statue hits me in the face and brings me back to life as I pull up in front of my house. I wonder if Louretta would be pissed if I just chopped off a pinky? That would pay for the funeral, and at least five or six whorehouse sessions—that's all I keep thinking as she hugs me when I walk into the house.

"How did it go? Did you pick out a nice casket?"

"Well, the good news is that it doesn't cost an arm and a leg, but it will probably cost a pinky."

"No! Absolutely not!"

"They took all of our gold and melted it onto our child. We have nothing left. How do you expect me to pay for it?"

"I don't know. You're the man of the house, figure it out. Dinner is ready."

I throw my cowboy hat against the wall in frustration. Women never fully realize that shit costs money. On the kitchen table I notice a giant bowl of cabbage stew. I'm now officially living in Poverty, USA.

Staring at my stew, I glance up at the now-empty gold shaker and see Sven's fat face pop up inside of it. He begins laughing at me again with that shit-eating grin. Just as I hit my breaking point, the worst thought I've ever had enters my mind.

Look, I've done a lot of fucked up things in my life, but this may be the worst. Shocked that I'm even considering this, I push my bowl of stew away from me and excuse myself from the table.

"I'm gonna go outside and have a smoke," I mumble.

Louretta doesn't even look at me as I leave. Grabbing my tin on the front porch, I roll myself a heater and stare straight ahead, directly at the outhouse. As I smoke, I think about how much gold we've all consumed as a family over time and how many times collectively we've all gone to the bathroom out there. There has to be a small fortune underneath that crapper. I take a long, deep drag on the cigarette and exhale knowingly. Fuck me.

Sometimes a man has to do what the fuck he has to do in order to survive. I light a lantern with my cigarette before taking one last drag. Unenthusiastically, I take off my shirt and tie it around my face, taking in one last deep breath before walking toward the out-house. Let it be known that today is the day I take shit into my own hands.

Chapter Seven

THE STRENGTH OF A MAN CAN ONLY BE MEASURED BY HOW MUCH HE CAN LIFT

The following morning I'm awakened by the sound of flies swarming inside a metal bucket next to me, as I lay sprawled out in the barn. The stench is so raw that I throw up within seconds. I cover my nose and look inside the bucket, seeing a stack of little chunks of gold covered in my family's shit. Sweet fucking Jesus, that wasn't a nightmare; I actually did this.

I stagger down to the river, grab a bucket of water, and rinse the remaining shit off with my fingers. There aren't a whole lot of words to express how vile and disgusting this is. When the gold is finally separated, I put the chunks inside a small leather pouch and tuck it in the pocket of my jeans. I bump into Louretta as she walks out of the house with a large basket full of laundry.

"Why did you sleep in the barn last night?" she asks.

"I had some shit to sort out. I'm going into town to go get the casket and post an obituary after I wash up."

She stares at me suspiciously. "How are you going to pay for the casket?"

"Don't worry. I'm a man, I figured it out. Go tell Daniel I want him to come with me after I take a bath, will you?"

She looks at me, surprised, and says, "Okay."

After I wash the shit off me, I head over to the barn to tie a covered wagon to my steed. Daniel runs out of the house excitedly. He's wearing jeans and cowboy boots, and holding his shirt, like a young motherfucking me.

"You wanted me to come with you, Dad?"

"Yeah, on three conditions. One, let's not be so fucking excited. We're going to pick out a casket for your dead brother, so let's ease up on the smiles. Two, start working out your pecs. Seven years old is the proper age to start getting ripped, so you should probably start an aggressive push-up routine as early as tomorrow. Three, do you know how to fire a gun? If not, it's time you learned. Get in."

I throw him down a holster with two pistols in it. He tries to suppress his excitement as he hops up into the wagon. Normally, I wouldn't take my kid with me into town, but this time I might need an extra man on the trigger.

An hour later, our wagon rolls down Main Street, and the first thing I see is a couple drunken Schläger brothers stumbling around. They point up at me and laugh. I stop the wagon and stand up, revealing my two pearl-handled pistols.

"Are we fucking doing this? Who wants to get wet?"

The two drunken brothers immediately back down. Daniel looks shaken, but I notice his right hand tapping one of his guns. This little fucker is clutch, and I like his heart. Someone like Ron, his first instinct would have been to hide in the covered wagon, throw a scarf around his face, and fake a British accent in a woman's voice like Mrs. Doubtfire to avoid the sitch. Not my boy. I snap the reins on my steed, and we continue riding to Curly's Funeral Parlor. Daniel looks up at me as we pull in.

"Those men looked like the guys who killed Totally Fucking Mexico."

"They were. Those are the Schläger brothers."

"Why didn't you kill them?"

"There are at least fifteen more of them. I don't want to have to put another son in the ground for at least another year. Your mom couldn't handle that."

"Fuck that shit, Dad. We can take them."

"I like your language. We'll have our revenge soon enough. Come on, I want to introduce you to a bald man named Curly."

As we walk into the parlor, Curly greets us with a wave and rubs his head again like we're old bros. He pulls a stick of rock candy out of his pocket that is covered in lint and hands it to Daniel. What is it with old people and hard candy? They love that shit as much as magic tricks. Curly kneels down to Daniel and pinches his face.

"Is this your boy, Saint James?"

"No, the dead one is at home. This is another one of my kids: Daniel."

Curly leans down to eye level with Daniel and says, "Hey, Daniel, you wanna see a magic trick?"

What did I tell you? Fucking magic tricks. I tell Daniel to fake a smile and go along with it, because I respect old people. This guy was probably on the *Mayflower* or some shit, so I nudge Daniel, who looks up at him and nods eagerly.

"Oh, yes sir! I'd love to see a magic trick!"

"Okay, watch the casket!" Curly walks over to the first adult-sized casket along the wall and opens it, revealing that there is nothing inside it. He then closes it quickly and pulls a wand out of his pocket.

"Abracadabra!" he says as he taps it with his wand.

Curly opens up the casket again, and we see a giant clown jump out holding a live cobra. Daniel screams his face off and runs out the front door as Curly laughs. Even I don't know what the fuck to say. The clown laughs hysterically, then walks toward the back, shuffling his plastic shoes along the way.

"Who is that?"

Curly laughs and says, "That's *my* son. He's hilarious. They grow up so fast; hard to believe he's forty-nine."

"How long has he been hiding in there?"

"About fourteen or fifteen hours. Totally worth it. You should have seen your faces! Anyhoo, you here for the caskets?"

"I'm sure as fuck not here for a cobra. I'll take the two that we were talking about yesterday."

I pull out my leather pouch full of gold nuggets and flip him a small chunk. Curly catches it and holds it up toward the light, examining it. He looks at it suspiciously, then turns back toward me.

"You know, it looks like gold, but it smells like shit."

"Since my boy died, I hide all of my gold up my own ass. You can't be too careful these days. Sorry."

"No need to apologize. My wife does the same thing with all her jewelry after I leave the house every morning."

We laugh and share a moment. Curly is a weird fucker, but I dig his spirit. Peering out the front door, I see Daniel hiding underneath my wagon outside.

"Curly, will you grab my boy and load the caskets up for me? I need to head down to the printing press to give them my son's obituary to run for the funeral proceedings."

"Of course. Before you go, I want you to pick a card," Curly says as he pulls a deck of cards out of his suit pocket. Begrudgingly I pull one out.

"Okay, got it."

"Put it back in the deck and remember it. I'll tell you what it was when you get back!"

"Can't wait."

I find myself with new life in my step as I head down to Ron's place of business. I'm excited to see the beating I gave him. From the street, I notice a sign on Ron's office door that says "Out to Lunch," but I see that fat little pigshit eating a sandwich alone in the back. There's no way he'd go out and face the public for lunch after what I did to him. I knock loudly on the window to get his attention.

"I see you, Ron! Let me in, or else I'll fucking drag you out into the street and beat you for all to see!"

When I start to unbuckle my belt, Ron bolts upright from his chair and scurries toward the door. He quivers at the sight of the sunlight; his face is more swollen than Quasimodo in *The Hunchback of Notre Dame*. I smile at him with an "I fucked your wife" look on my face.

"Hi, Ron, you look well. Can I come in? I need you to print an obituary for my dead kid. You know, the one that you did nothing to help from being murdered?"

"Okay. Just please promise you won't hurt me."

"The only thing I can promise is that I won't fuck your wife today if you do what I ask. Now open the fucking door."

Ron obliges and lets me in. He walks me to the back of the shop where his workbench is set up. Newspapers are strewn everywhere, and his hands are stained with ink. It's depressing as shit in here. I bet Ron keeps a pet mouse in a shoebox and takes it out and feeds it sandwich crusts while they talk about great literary works.

As Ron clears some old newspapers off a chair for me to sit down in, I notice a handful of breadcrumbs under his desk. I fucking knew it.

"So do you have an obit prepared, or do you want me to write something?" he asks.

"Well, Ron, obituaries are never really *prepared*, but yes, I have something written down."

I pull a small note out of my pocket and hand it to him. "Please read this aloud."

Beads of sweat start to form around his temples as he clears his throat. "Saint James, I can't—"

"Read it with precision and passion, Ron! Word for fucking word!"

"Fine. God."

"Totally Fucking Mexico Street James. Born sometime in 1849ish, I think. Died July 18, 1853. Totally Fucking Mexico was four, and he didn't get to do a lot of shit, so obviously his résumé isn't that impressive. He was well hung, a trait he inherited from his father. Just like his dad, he had trouble keeping his dong inside a cloth diaper as a baby. He loved to eat gold, so it's ironic that he died being dipped in it. Our bitch neighbor 'Ron' did nothing to stop the gruesome attack and let him die. Ron paid the ultimate price for that, believe me. Totally Fucking Mexico is survived by his six brothers; mother, Louretta; and his father/loving husband/mentor of young women between the ages of eighteen and twenty-five/gunfighter/sexual provocateur, Saint James Street James. A memorial service is scheduled for Saturday at 2 PM at the Street James estate. It's potluck, so bring a dish— a real dish—don't be the asshole that brings only bread or a fucking condiment. Clothing optional for women. BYOB too. Park your carriages wherever."

"What do you think?" I ask him.

"Um, it's good. Do you have to put the part in there about the 'bitch neighbor'?"

"Yes, it's mandatory. You're lucky I didn't write the part about me fucking your wife in there. Have a nice day, Ron."

On the way out, I fake a backhand slap toward Ron just to keep him fearful of me. He cowers like a sniveling bitch. I shake my head and grin at him.

"I want that obit done in a timely manner. Don't spend all day making tiny business suits for your fucking mouse."

"Mr. Wiggins is a hamster—"

I slam the door in his face. The second I leave, he immediately locks it and slumps down to the floor. I can hear him sobbing and whispering prayers in Latin.

Down the street, I notice Daniel and Curly struggling to load the two heavy caskets into the wagon. I'm sure they got it. A whore passes by me and whistles, as I feel the gold in my leather pouch shake in my jeans. She's a four in the daylight, with the highest possible score being a six in extreme darkness after an entire bottle of pick-your-fucking-choice. Normally I wouldn't even consider her, but I've got some time to burn.

She grabs my dick over my jeans, leans in, and says, "Heard about your kid. I'm really sorry. You need to take a load off, specifically in my mouth?"

"How much?"

"A quarter ounce of Au."

I point to a large piece of plywood on the ground with a decent-sized hole in it. "Okay, but grab this plywood, wait two minutes, and meet me in the back alley."

A couple minutes later she walks back, awkwardly holding the plywood. I stand it upright on the ground and instruct her to kneel behind it on the other side. She looks at me, puzzled.

"Why?"

"It's obviously because I can't bear to look at your face."

"Fair enough."

Surprisingly, she gets where I'm coming from. I unzip my pants, stick my dick through the hole, and fellatio ensues in broad daylight.

Side note, there's nothing better than a blowjob from a four. They've always had to overcompensate their whole lives, so they know how to suck a dick. A group of butchers slaughtering a cow stop mid-slice and walk out of their shop to see what's going on.

"Hey, man, what the hell are you doing?" one of them asks.

"I'm getting my dick sucked through this hole."

"Why?"

"She's a four."

They all nod knowingly. "Smart. That all makes total sense. Have a good one," one of them says.

The hooker stops blowing me for a second and turns around. "If you boys want, you can all line up and stick your dicks through the hole. I'll suck off all of you for the same price!"

It's hard to turn down a cheap beej, even from a four. A line quickly begins to form behind me. Look, I've invented a lot of great things in my life, but to this day, I'm still most proud of inventing the first glory hole.* After we all get sucked off, we laugh and share a bottle of whiskey together. At the heart of it, a glory hole is a communal entity that is meant to be enjoyed by a group.

Our jovial celebration is cut short by the sounds of gunshots, followed by a loud scream. I race around the corner and see a dead clown shot in the chest, lying facedown in the street in front of my wagon. It's Curly's son. His eyes are closed, but ironically there

---

* I even applied for a patent on it, but the patent office said it would be difficult to enforce since "anyone could cut a hole in anything and suck a dick through it." For personal pride, though, I want it on the record that I did indeed invent this.

are open eyes painted *on top* of his eyelids. It's pretty fucking creepy.

The two drunk Schläger brothers from earlier are tugging on the coffins, trying to rip them out of my covered wagon. I see Daniel lying on top protecting them from being taken.

"Give us these coffins, boy! We're gonna bury you and your daddy alive!" one of them shouts.

The other Schläger pulls out a gun and aims it at Daniel. I quick-draw my pistols and shoot both of them down in the street. Pedestrians scramble and run for cover as I run over to Daniel. Moments later, Curly comes running out of the funeral parlor. His face is painted like a sad clown with fake tears streaming down his cheeks. He leans down and holds his dead son in his arms, screaming skyward.

"Why did you have to take him? Whyyyyyyyyyyy?"

Suddenly, Daniel's eyes grow wide. He pulls out both of his guns and aims them slightly to the sides of my head, firing two shots behind me. I turn to see two more Schläger brothers fall to the street, dead. In the distance I see the remaining thirteen coming out of the whorehouse.

Within moments, we're about to be in an all-out street war. Imagine being in the middle of a gunfight against seventeen dudes and realizing that your only backup is an almost-eight-year-old boy who has just fired a gun for the first time in his life and a seventy-year-old man with his face painted like a sad clown. Holy shit, we're fucked . . . *or so I thought*. I am about to learn firsthand what "old-man strength" is.

For you novices, old-man strength is something that can't be taught. It's not something you're born with. There is no amount of weight you can lift to achieve it. And it's the only thing in this world that can't be bought. Old-man strength is a certain strength that is acquired over a long period of time, typically by men who have seen some hard-ass shit in their day. The Pilgrims had it. Men of the Revolutionary War had it. The men of the gold rush *definitely* have it, mixed in with a dash of insanity as well. There is nothing to do out here, so you do any fucked-up thing you can think of to fight off the boredom of living in mostly undeveloped land. Only one thing in this world trumps old-man strength, but we'll get to that in a minute.

Curly shows me exactly what old-man strength truly is. With the Schläger brothers rapidly approaching, I draw my own guns and look over at Curly to warn him of the imminent danger. He nods and shakes his head with a look of rage I have rarely seen in a man's eyes. Kneeling down, he kisses the forehead of his dead clown son.

"Grab your boy and stand back," he says to me in a deep, guttural voice.

With that kind of look in his eyes, I don't even question him. I grab Daniel out of the back of the wagon and pull him down to the ground. Faster than a goose shits, Curly unhooks my steed from the wagon, then grabs a wheel and lifts the entire thing up above his head. He flips it over on its side, shielding us from the Schläger brothers' line of fire. That's old-man strength, son. That wagon probably weighs four hundred pounds, and that motherfucker just deadlifts it without even chalking up first.

I tell my steed to run for cover as the three of us sit behind the wagon as shots are continuously fired at us. Curly pulls out two sawed-off street howitzers and begins loading shells from his vest pockets. He doesn't even look while he's loading; instead he's focused on us. I don't even know where the guns were hidden on him, that's how fucking boss he is.

"Cover me, I'm going out there!"

"You can't go out there alone, Curly, there's too many men, god-damn it!"

"They just killed my only son, Saint James. I don't have anything else to live for now. Either you're in or you're out."

I look over at Daniel and nod, then say, "The Street James boys are in."

He nods back appreciatively, then slowly stands up from behind the wagon and walks out into the middle of the street. The Schläger brothers stop firing for a second and admire the bravado of this man. Also, it's pretty fucking shocking to see a seventy-year-old dude painted like a sad clown walking down the street with two loaded shotguns. Curly pulls the hammers back with his thumbs and yells, "These are the tears of a clown, motherfuckers!"

He unloads both shotguns into the chests of two brothers. In unison, Daniel and I stand up and start blasting the shit out of as many brothers as we can. Curly recocks and blows the fuck out of two more as we keep firing. Six brothers are down, but there are eight more left, and Curly is out of ammo. Sven steps out of the shadows with a huge smile on his face. He pulls a shotgun out of his overcoat and aims it at Curly. Daniel and I try to fire at him, but we're out of bullets too. All we can do is stand there and watch as Sven takes his time cocking his gun.

"Let's turn that frown upside down," he says.

Sven calmly blows Curly away with a shotgun blast to the stomach, which causes him to fly backward out of his boots. No lie, the man is *physically blown out of his boots*. As I watch his shoeless body fly back in the air, all I keep thinking is what a shitty line that is to die to. The last thing this hardcore SOB dies to is a phrase that was used by a local toy store down the street? Fuck that. Curly deserves better, and I'll be goddamned if I'm going to let him go out like that. I reload as quickly as I can and ask Daniel for his guns so I can reload his as well.

"Come on out, Saint James! I'll tell you what. If you come out peacefully and surrender, we'll just hang you and let your boy go. Hell, for all you've done for this town, we might even name this here road after you. Main Street James has a nice ring to it!"

My temp begins to rise. Now he's trying to kill me to a shitty pun as well? Nope. Not this guy. And not in this fucking lifetime. Sven fires a shot at me as I try to steal a quick glance over the top of the wagon. I duck at the last second, narrowly avoiding it. As I observe my surroundings, there's only one way out of this, and it ain't pretty. I walk out into the street and start firing with both guns blazing, trying to take out as many as I can.

Daniel's voice suddenly cries out, "I got your back, Dad!"

"Stay there, Daniel!"

By the time I look back toward him, he's already sprinted out in front of me in the street, blasting both guns. This crazy son of a bitch wasn't kidding; he's using himself as a human shield. We're killing a lot of Schlägers, but Daniel is getting lit up faster than a spliff on April 20 at 4:19 PM. As a father, it's a hopeless feeling when you realize there's nothing you can do to help your child in a moment like this. At least I bought two caskets, so I'm cool on that front.

I scoop up his lifeless body and retreat behind a large wooden post in front of Curly's Parlor. Peering out, I see only one Schläger still standing, and it's Sven. He fires a shot at me that hits the post and ricochets off into the distance. I lean down and kiss Daniel good-bye on the forehead and look up toward Sven, filled with the same rage Curly had. One-on-one, this man is going to fucking die, so I might as well put on a display of dominance for the entire town.

"Seven, it looks like it's just me and you now. How about we just settle this out in the middle of the street like gentlemen?"

"That's fine by me! And it's *Sven*, by the way. You keep throwing an extra *e* in there!"

"Really? I'm not hearing it."

Once I'm finally reloaded, I peek out from behind the post and see him slowly walking out toward the middle of the street, where I casually join him. Patrons also start to walk out of businesses and line up to see this epic showdown. Sixteen dead Schläger brothers litter the street, and Sven and I are literally stepping over bodies to get closer to one another.

We eventually end up about twenty yards apart before we stop. Staring each other down, both of us put one hand on our guns. I notice a slight twitch in Sven's right index finger. It's evident that he's nervous from everything he's heard about me. I would be too. Time to add water and make my legend grow.

"I tell you what; you can have the first shot," I say to him.

The entire crowd that has gathered gasps collectively. Women swoon. Other men's dicks get hard, because they wish they could do shit like this. I tear off my shirt for good measure, to get one more set of gasps from the ladies in the crowd. Three different women faint; one gets her period.

"You can't be serious," he says in shock.

"Only one way to find out. Better make this shot count, *Seven*."

I raise my hands slowly above my head away from my guns, but still flexing my abs. With all eyes fixated on Sven, he quick-draws his gun and fires at me. I don't even fucking blink as the shot hits me in the leg. Blood spurts out of my thigh and I begin to laugh. Sven's eyes fill with fear.

"Oh shit . . ."

"Goodbye, Seven."

Before Sven can get off another shot, I quick-draw my gun on the left side and throw it up high in the air. With Sven's attention diverted to the flight of my spinning gun, I quick-draw my right pistol and shoot the spinning gun's trigger, causing it to fire a bullet right through Sven's head. He falls over dead on the ground, staring straight ahead. The entire crowd groans in delight.

I blow kisses to the crowd and give a double crotch chop with my hands, playing to my fans, before limping over to pick up my own gun. Out of nowhere a huge barbarian of a man tackles me from behind, knocking the wind out of me as I hit the dirt. He flips me over on my back and punches me in face with one of the hardest shots I've ever taken in my entire life. I try to gather my bearings, but I'm immediately rocked again in the face by his other fist. When I try to cover up, I'm hit with two more punches from different arms. What the hell is happening? I squint through my defense and see that this beast has a third arm growing out of his chest! His eyes are off center and spaced way too far apart.

"You killed my brothers!" he says in a deep, delayed lisp.

Oh fuck. As soon as I hear that voice, panic washes over me. Remember earlier when I said there is only one thing that trumps old-man strength? Welcome to "retard strength." That's not a euphemism for anything; I'm talking about the strength of a mentally or physically retarded adult male. There is nothing else in this world that compares to their kind of strength. That kind of power is just downright fucking scary. God threw them a bone by providing that kind of strength. I'll even go so far as to say that they *deserve* to be that strong. When you have that much incest going on inside of one family like the Schlägers do, a human mutation is bound to happen, and right now this three-armed Toxic Avenger man-child is locked in.

The arm that has grown from his chest is choking me, while his other two hit me in the face with a series of right/left combos. I have no chance of reaching my gun. Just when I'm about to black out—*bang!*—a lone gunshot rings out and pierces the heart of the beast. He slumps over facedown on top of me. In the distance I see smoke rising from Daniel's gun. Miraculously, he's somehow still alive.

I throw the dead retard off me and limp over to Daniel. His little body is riddled with bullet holes. As he coughs up blood all over the place, I grab his hand. He tries to smile through clenched teeth as he looks up at me, but he's shaking pretty badly.

"Did I do good, Dad?"

"You did real good, son. If I'm being picky, you could have killed him a little sooner, though. I took a lot of shots."

"*You* did? Look at me!" A warm father-son laugh ensues as he coughs up more blood, sensing the inevitable. I squeeze his hand as he looks down at his blood-soaked clothes and asks, "Am I going to die?"

"No. You're a fucking Street James. It takes more than sixty-three shots to kill a Street James. Do you hear me?"

He tries to smile and nods his little head. "I think I see Totally Fucking Mexico."

"It's just an illusion. The way the sun catches his statue, everyone in town can probably see him. You stay with me and keep your eyes open, okay?"

Daniel tries to keep them open with all of his might, but they slowly close and his head falls back as I hold him in my arms.

"I need a fucking doctor!"

A man in a suit holding a doctor's bag sprints over. "I'm a doctor."

"Oh, thank God. My boy has been shot. I think he's dead. You gotta help me."

"Looks like you were hit too," he says as he points down at my leg, which is still shooting out blood. "Here, drink this." He pulls out a small, brown medicine bottle, and I take a swig.

"Holy shit, this is strong. What's in it?"

"It's a new medicine called laudanum that contains opium. I got it from a Chinese doctor, and no one knows the side effects of it, so go easy."

I've already pounded half the bottle before the doctor finishes his sentence. I pick up Daniel and load him into the doc's carriage. As we head off, I look out at the carnage strewn in the street as we ride away. I see Curly lying faceup, blood covering most of his face paint. Through weary eyes, I see him slowly come to life and pull something out of a bullet wound in his chest. He tries to grin as he proudly holds up a nine of diamonds.

"Was this the card you picked?" he asks in a whisper.

"No. Sorry, Curly."

He nods in disappointment, and his head falls back, dead on the ground. Truthfully, it *is* my card, but I hate magic so much that I'm not even willing to give a dying man one more smile. If he was a real magician, he could bring himself back to life right now. Guess who doesn't open his eyes ever again?

Chapter Eight

DEATH IS A HEAVY THING . . . ESPECIALLY WHEN THE CORPSE WEIGHS MORE THAN EIGHT HUNDRED POUNDS

I awake to see the doctor standing over me, snapping his fingers in front of my face, staring at me intently. It takes me a moment to assess my surroundings, but finally I recognize that I'm at home in my own bed. My leg has been bandaged where I got shot, and my cock is tied down to my other leg. Obviously, it was a preventive measure so the doc wouldn't be knocked unconscious by a stray boner while tending to my well-being.

"How are you feeling, Mr. Street James?"

"Pretty fucking shitty, dude."

"Well, I don't mean to pull my pants down and dump out on you any more, but there's a rumor in town that the law is coming for you."

"What law? We don't have fucking law in this town?"

Louretta walks in hurriedly, wearing a long black dress. "Good, you're finally awake. Get dressed, people will be arriving for the funeral soon."

"The funeral is Saturday. How long have I been sleeping?"

"Three days," she says flatly.

"Awesome. Doc, I'm *definitely* going to need more of that laudanum."

"I've left four bottles for you and your son."

"Daniel is *alive*? Where is he?"

"He's sleeping in his room. It's a miracle. He was shot sixty-three times. I've never seen anything like it."

"Well, let's not forget that I was shot too."

Louretta shakes her head and says, "Daniel's not saying what happened, so maybe you can fill me in on why our son was shot sixty-three times and you were only shot once?"

"He's not really that nimble?"

"Lovely. Help me put the food out for the funeral. It starts in twenty minutes, so get up."

As she walks the doctor out, I rise up out of bed buck naked and limp over to the window, where I see people starting to arrive out front. I spot Ron and Sheila pulling up on their gimpy horse, so I pull the curtain all the way back and make sure they both see me in all my glory. Sheila waves at me, and I salute her back by smacking my dong against the window. Once I'm satisfied with Ron's level of discomfort, I take a swig of laudanum and begin to get dressed.

Getting dressed for your own son's funeral is really tough. As a parent, it's something you never prepare yourself for. Staring into my closet full of suits, I want something that says, "This motherfucker is hard but isn't trying too much." I finally decide on an all-black ensemble made entirely out of bison skin, accessorized with bison-skin boots.

As I limp down the stairs, I see that Louretta has everything beautifully organized. I stuff a fistful of deviled eggs into my face on my way outside to greet everyone. Standing in the sweltering heat waiting for me are the town preacher, Pastor Jenkins; my remaining sons; and Ron. Pastor Jenkins, who is super fucking old, looks up at me hesitantly before finally raising his hand.

"Speak, your high power," I instruct him.

"Saint James, I don't know how to tell you this, but we're going to need some extra pallbearers."

"Why?"

"Your son weighs more than eight hundred pounds."

"Shit, I forgot about that. Typically that amount of weight wouldn't be a problem for me to carry on my own, but with *me being shot in the leg*, I can't get any lift out of my quads. Are there any more dudes here?"

"Just a few boys from the blind school down the road. We could yell out our steps in unison," Pastor Jenkins meekly says.

"I wish I could *unhear* what you just said. Jesus, man. All right, I guess everyone is going to have to man the fuck up today. I'll do the heavy lifting at the front. Everyone else fall behind. Ron, don't you dare let that back end fall, or it's your ass!"

I spit in my hands, then chalk up over by the porch. Yes, I keep chalk out in front of my house for when I have to lift heavy shit. Curly was a freak of nature, lifting that wagon without chalking up. Full disclosure, I don't have old-man strength right now; instead I just possess a lot of God-given raw, natural power. Plus I'm on opium, so I could probably lift a fucking bank vault.

After a sweet chalk sesh, I lift the casket up with ease, and everyone falls in behind me, holding up the back. We walk toward the big oak tree down by the river, while Louretta starts playing a set of seventeenth-century bagpipes that her parents brought over from Ireland. A smattering of people begin weeping, including Sheila. Another woman in the front row starts peeling potatoes by hand, which is apparently a tradition at Irish funerals.

With only about ten yards remaining in our walk, I feel the back half of the casket slipping. Behind me I hear grunting and labored breathing. Turning back, I see Ron's arms shaking, desperately trying to hold up the casket. *Gong!* It falls to the ground, and everyone gasps, including Louretta, who blows out a bagpipe and starts crying hysterically.

"Goddamn it, Ron! What the fuck did I tell you?"

"No, you're right. I totally deserve this one," he says as he gets on all fours and assumes a beating position.

The pastor runs over and grabs my arm after I've already taken off my belt. "You don't want to do this here, Saint James."

"No, I definitely do. Why don't you take your goddamn hand off me and go put one foot in that grave."

"Saint James! This day is about Totally Mexico!" Louretta cries out.

I see the tears in her eyes and decide to postpone Ron's beating. Instead, I take a pull of laudanum and lift up the casket "fireman's carry" style, over my shoulder, walking it over on my own. People clap for my bravery as I lower it into the pre-dug grave. One woman even flashes me her beaver when I walk up to give my eulogy.

"What can I say about our beloved son Totally Fucking Mexico Street James that hasn't already been said? He was a magical boy with big hopes and dreams? He was destined to change the world? His unique vision and outlook on life were things to be cherished by all who met him? Well, I can't really say that, because he was taken from us at four years old, so who knows what the fuck he was thinking about. What I can tell you is that he had two arms and two legs. Ten fingers, and ten toes. He had blond hair and a pretty ripped physique for a four-year-old. He loved to spend his free time, which was *all* the time, playing outside with my freshly sharpened axes, swimming in the river with heavy rocks tied to his legs, or just fooling around in our knife drawer in the kitchen. Normal kid stuff, you know? That little son of a bitch had a heart of gold that was only eclipsed by his golden spirit. So today, as his tiny little body gets lowered into the ground forever, I want you all to take solace in the fact that the men who did this were killed in brutal fashion also. All seventeen of them were shot dead by me, a seventy-year-old man painted as a sad clown, and another of my sons, Daniel, who was shot sixty-three times in the altercation. I'm proud of you, Daniel, for killing that retard."

I point up to Daniel, who sits in a full-body cast with his legs stuffed outside the window. He nods and tips his bottle of laudanum toward me, and we cheers.

"I know what you're thinking: doesn't senseless violence breed *more* senseless violence? To those people thinking that bullshit, I ask you, is touch not a sense? Because right now my dead son will never get to be touched again. Not by his family, not by a woman, and certainly not by a stranger who just wants to party. So keep your thoughts to yourself, and don't ever voice them if you're thinking about shit like that. If you want to ask me how many fucks I give that those men are dead, the answer is zero. Did I kill one or two of them first? Probably. Shit gets wild sometimes when grown men are drinking. That's not an excuse to kill an innocent child. If you have a problem, handle it man-to-man."

I wink at Ron, who looks away.

"Mentally, my wife and I are going to be really fucked up for years and years to come, but that's what life is. It's overcoming tragedy by inflicting it on someone else. I'd like to close my eulogy with one solitary wish for my special tiny dancer. TFM, may you never know the pain of chafing ever again, for in heaven, your sweet nuts will forever be cradled by the powdery hands of angels."

I cup my hands together and blow kisses to the crowd with the remaining chalk dust on my palms. Everyone stands up and erupts in applause; there's not a dry eye in the house. Pastor Jenkins asks everyone to bow their heads in a moment of silence. As they bow, I walk over to Totally Fucking Mexico's open casket and pull out a mallet I have stuffed in the back of my pants and bang it on the statue, which invokes the sound of a church bell ringing. After the fourth and final *gong*, one for every year of his life, I take one last sip from my bottle of laudanum . . . *which proves to be a little too much.*

There are a lot of questions surrounding what happens next. Most people think that I am so stricken with grief that I hurl myself onto his casket, but in truth, I black out and fall on top of it. I can feel people throwing roses and potato peelings on top of me as they pass by. The one thing I can be sure of is, for the first time in my life, I am truly grieving.

After an hour of my being blacked out on top of the casket, Louretta leaves me there and continues the reception inside. I probably would stay there all night, if I weren't awakened by the woman who flashed me her beaver during my eulogy. She is now standing over me with her legs spread wide apart, straddling both sides of the grave, whispering down to me.

"Hey! Hey! Look up here. Can you see my vagina?"

I open my eyes. "Of course, you're not wearing any panties. I can see your whole birth canal."

"Good. Do you want to screw?"

I nod my head yes, and she climbs down inside the grave with me. I may be groggy as shit, but I can recognize a sweet beave anywhere. Within seconds, she unzips my pants, puts my cowboy hat on her head, and jams my dick inside her. I move my hand up her dress and squeeze her tits as she rides me, slowly starting to come to life. Now that I'm fully awake with the realization of where I'm at, I stop her.

"What's wrong?" she asks.

"*This*. We're fucking on top of my dead kid's casket. I've done a lot of horrific shit in my life, but this takes the quadriplegic's cake."

"Does it? Or is this the ultimate send-off? What better way to feel alive again than to have sex on *top* of death? Your son would want this."

Wow. This woman is fucking crazy, but she makes a great point. I don't even have a counterargument, so I shrug my shoulders and let her continue. She grabs my hands and slams them down on the casket above my head.

"Just lay there and grieve for me, baby," she whispers.

She picks up her pace, and little chunks of dirt from inside the grave begin falling all around us. I'm not going to lie, this really *is* helping me grieve, and I'm actually starting to get emotional about it. I look up toward the sky and see Totally Fucking Mexico's spirit running around the grave in circles with my steed. The two of them are laughing. This strange gypsy woman, combined with all this laudanum, has taken me to a different planet.

When I climax, it feels like a euphoric rainbow is shooting out of my dick hole. She clutches a fistful of roses and orgasms *after* me, which is a first. The thorns on the stems cause her hands to bleed, and she holds them over my mouth, letting her blood drip down into it.

"*This* is fucking life!" she moans.

I look into her eyes and scream, "*Mi vida loca!*"

A strange man peeks his head into the grave and destroys my moment of unadulterated bliss. He has a gun drawn, aiming it at my head. I go to grab my own guns, but my pants are down around my ankles.

"Are you Saint James Street James?"

"You can see my dick and balls, can't you? Of course I'm him." I get up and pull my pants back up. "Who the fuck are you?"

He smiles and pulls out a copper badge. "I'm the new sheriff in town, and you're wanted for murder. Leave the guns and put these on."

He throws down a pair of handcuffs, which I properly throw back at him. "Let me get out of my dead son's grave first, asshole."

As the strange gypsy woman and I climb out of the grave, I notice the entire reception has stopped and come outside. Louretta stands on the front porch watching me and who I believe to be her friend dusting the dirt off our clothes. A look of disgust and confusion washes over her face.

"What the hell is going on?" she asks.

"I'm Sheriff Madsen, and this man is wanted for multiple murders. I was appointed by US Marshals this morning to curb the violence in this town, so I'm taking him in. Put the cuffs on, sir."

"Or what?" I ask.

He draws his other gun and points it at me as well. "You're wanted dead or alive. It's your choice."

"All right. I choose *your* death."

I look up at Daniel, who has a street howitzer aimed at the sheriff. The sheriff's eyes grow wide with fear at the sight of a young boy in a full-body cast holding a shotgun. Although you can barely see his face from inside the cast, you can make out his smile. *Boom!* He pulls the trigger, blasting the sheriff square in the chest. The entire reception retreats in horror as he hits the ground bleeding. I kneel down next to him.

"Don't ever try to arrest someone at their son's funeral. Ever. On the positive side, though, you won't be able to tell my wife that I was fucking that weird girl on top of his casket. Rest in peace, spider-cock."

As the sheriff takes his last breath, he holds out his hand for me to hold, and I casually spit in it. This isn't a fucking cotillion, holmes. His head falls back on the ground, and he dies. I then kick his dead body, because why the fuck not?

"Everyone, please continue to grieve. Ron, come dig a grave for this bastard. There's a shovel out in the barn."

Ron shakes his head and says, "You know the marshals will come looking for you after this."

"You can wake up tomorrow in your bed or in a ditch, Ron; it's your choice. So shut the fuck up and go dig a grave for this asshole. Oh, and fill in the dirt on Totally Fucking Mexico's grave too, while you're at it. That will make up for your casket failure earlier, and we'll call it evesies."

Walking up to the house, I wink at Daniel up in the window, and he winks back as he puts down the shotgun. The kid is quickly becoming my favorite son. Not only did he take sixty-three shots like a boss, but now he's icing other people who threaten me. Louretta stops me on the porch on my way in.

"When is the killing going to stop, Saint James?"

"I don't know. I don't have anyone on tap for tonight, so I guess *now*? There's always the off chance Ron gets out of line and decides to grow a pair, so maybe *him*, but that's probably it."

"Do you want more of your family to get killed? Is that it?"

"Everything I do is to protect this family. I'm gonna go upstairs and check on our son who was shot sixty-three times." I grab the remaining tray of deviled eggs and head up the stairs.

With the sun setting, I pull up a chair and sit next to Daniel. Both sets of our legs dangle out the upstairs window, his obviously set in a body cast. We drink laudanum together and watch the sun go down. From up here, I can tell that he was definitely watching me fuck that weird girl in the grave. He offers me any part of his cast to wipe her blood off my face from the roses. I oblige with his right arm.

Whenever people tell me that I'm not a good father, I often tell them of this moment. This is way better than teaching him to ride one of those bicycles with the huge tire in the front and a tiny one in the back. I put my arm around his body cast, and we quietly nod off together in a drug-fueled haze.

Chapter Nine

THERE ARE LAWS NOW? WHAT THE FUCK?

The following morning I wake up to the vibrant sounds of birds chirping and a warm summer breeze blowing across my face. I have my arm around my son, and there's urine all over the hardwood floor from both of us blacking out on laudanum last night. This tranquil moment is suddenly interrupted by two sets of shotgun blasts.

Out in the yard, I see thirty US Marshals on horseback with their guns pointed at the house. I hear the *click* of Daniel's shotgun as he wakes up too.

"Saint James Street James, we have a warrant for your arrest for the murder of a sheriff and nineteen Schläger brothers! Come out with your hands up, or we will burn the house down," one of the marshals yells out.

"We can take them, Dad," Daniel says with a slight opium slur.

"Probably, but they would kill the rest of our family."

"I'm willing to take that risk if you are."

Louretta comes running in holding our youngest son. "Saint James, there's a bunch of US Marshals outside, and they say they're going to burn the house down if you don't come out! Jesus, did you two piss yourselves?"

"It appears so. Can you mop this up after I leave? I'm going to let them take me in after I take a bath."

"Dad, no!" Daniel says.

"I have to, Daniel. I don't want anything else to happen to you guys. Don't worry, it will probably be a slap on the dick, and then they'll let me go. Here, take this." With pride, I hand him my bottle of laudanum and stand up.

"Are you coming out or not, Saint James?" another marshal yells.

I stick my head out of the window and yell down, "Yeah, I'm coming out. Just give me a quick forty-five to wash off my privates."

The marshals all look at each other, confused.

"As a show of good faith, I'm going to throw down my guns, okay?"

The marshals nod as I unbuckle my holster and hold my guns up. When I toss the holster out the window, it takes a weird hop off the roof and the guns hit the ground. They both fire simultaneously, killing two more marshals. Their two bodies slump over, falling off their horses and onto the dirt.

"You just killed fraternal twins, Saint James!" another marshal screams.

"Shit. Sorry. Total accident. I'm gonna wash up now."

"We're adding them to your murder count!"

"What-the-fuck-ever."

Before I take off my clothes and head for the bath, I kiss Louretta on the cheek and instruct her to paint the crotch area on Daniel's cast from yellow back to white. A parent's job is never done, you know?

An hour later, after a good cock soak, I depart the house with my hands in the air. The marshals approach me with their guns drawn and place the handcuffs on me. They pull one of their horses over and instruct me to get on it so they can lead me into town.

"Fuck that. I ride my own steed into town, or you're going to have more blood on your hands, you hear?"

Daniel whistles from above, his shotgun trained at them. With half his face now frozen from taking so much laudanum, he looks kind of crazy, so they decide to let me ride my steed. I give him a two-finger whistle, and on cue, he slow-trots out of the barn.

Looking back at the house, I see Lou standing out on the porch waving at me, surrounded by the rest of my kids. She mouths the words "Thank you." Daniel holds up the bottle of laudanum and pours out a sip in respect. It finally sets in that I'm really going to jail.

As we make our way through town, everyone stops and gawks at me surrounded by the marshals. I take it all in, knowing that this image of me riding to jail wearing handcuffs will only cause more people to fear me. The marshals' horses hit the end of Main Street and slowly come to a halt. Curiously, I've never been to this part of town before.

By "this part of town" I mean any building or structure past the whorehouse. This is a newly built jail at the end of the street, a block down from the whorehouse, so I haven't been here yet. A guy on a ladder is finishing painting the word "JAIL" on the building in black letters when the marshals ask me to get down from my steed.

"You want us to take your horse back to your house for you? You're going to be here for a while," one of the marshals says to me.

"No. He can find his way home if he chooses. Maybe he has a date in town tonight. I try not to put any limits on him."

"That's real funny. We'll see how funny you are from inside a jail cell."

"Do you guys need more time to paint the word 'cell' above it first?"

One of the marshals grabs me and leads me through the front door. On the way in, I shake my leg twice, and an apple rolls down my pant leg, resting on my boot. I kick it up in the air to my horse, who catches it midair in his mouth.

"You keep an apple tucked inside your jeans?" a marshal asks.

"I didn't know it was there until I stood up. My cock is like an elephant trunk; sometimes it just reaches up and grabs fruit unbeknownst to me."

"Come on, asshole," he says, leading me in.

Looking at the decor, you can tell that it was probably an old blacksmith shop before this. They throw me inside an old wrought-iron ten-by-fourteen-foot jail cell and slam the door. A janky bed, a bucket of water to wash up in, and a hole in the ground to piss and shit in are all that await me.

In the cell next to me, I see a fat Mexican man taking a grump in his hole while eating a half-open can of beans at the same time.

A few flies swarm around him, and the smell is making a mural of the Virgin Mary that he has painted above his bed cry. One of the marshals sees me shake my head in disgust.

"It's a miracle, isn't it, Saint James?" he says as he laughs and points at the painting.

"You ain't in that log mansion out in the woods anymore, are you, boy?" another one says.

I quickly pull out my Buck knife from the back of my jeans and whip it through the jail cell bars, pinning a marshal's shirt to the wall.

"Let me make one thing clear to you: if I wanted you dead, you'd be dead by now."

With that little reminder, I walk over to the bed and lie down.

"Keep an eye on him, Deputy. If he so much as shits wrong, shoot him," the marshal I pinned says.

"How does someone shit wrong?" I think to myself as the marshals leave. Suddenly the fat Mexican dude farts, and it sounds like a phone book is being ripped in half. The wall behind his makeshift toilet inside his cell is suddenly splattered like a can of chocolate syrup exploded in a campfire. I guess my question has been answered.

"How long am I going to be in here, Deputy?"

"There will be a trial in about a week or so," he says.

"What? I will be wearing your skin and pretending to be you if I'm in here that long."

"Nothing I can do about speeding up your trial."

"One word: 'conjugal.' Them shits better be allowed, then."

"I might be able to let that slide."

"Good. I'm sure I'll have a lot of visitors."

My steed peeks his snout through the bars of my window. I look up and see his sad eyes and stand up on my bed, leaning into him, nose-to-nose. When he exhales, I inhale. That's how fucking close we are.

"It's been a real fuckery of a last couple days, hasn't it? Why don't you go home and get some rest."

He shakes his head no. "Sshhhhhhh, I'm going to be fine. The children need you. Plus I smuggled a full bottle of *this* in," I say, pulling a bottle of laudanum out of my boot and waving it in front of his face. He neighs with excitement.

"Now go on and get your big beautiful dick out of here."

He nods and slowly trots off. As I watch him ride away, he stops and lifts his front legs in the air and neighs as loud as possible up toward the heavens. I swear to God, I'd rather lose another kid than lose my steed.

The following morning I am awakened by the deputy, telling me that I have a visitor. As my eyes adjust to the sun, I see the Mexican shitting. Again.

"Hey, Chubs, you shit in that hole one more time today, and I'm going to bury you in it. *Comprende*?" I say to him sternly.

"What am I supposed to do if I have to go to the bathroom?"

I reach into my jeans pocket, pull out a small sewing kit, and toss it to him. "You better start sewing your asshole shut. Cheek to cheek. A classic backstitch should work."

He looks at me defeated as the deputy walks back with my first visitor. To my surprise, it's Sheila, and she's carrying a picnic basket. She is definitely not the first woman I was expecting to come visit me, but she'll do. I haven't had sex in almost twelve hours, so obviously my jeans can barely contain my cock right now.

To her credit, Sheila looks prettier than usual, and a lot more done up than the last time I saw her. She squeezes the bars of the jail cell with her free hand and softly cries. I get up out of bed and walk over to comfort her.

"Why are you crying? Does seeing me behind bars make you sad?"

"No, it's not that. The smell in here is so horrific, I feel like my eyes are melting."

I look over at the fat Mexican and shake my head. "What? I'm doing it!" He screams as he lies down on his small bed and begins sewing his ass cheeks together with the sewing kit I gave him.

"Hopefully this stink will clear out soon, Sheila."

"I'm just worried about my tear ducts returning to normal," she says, as she wipes her eyes.

"I'm not a doctor, so I can't promise you anything. What are you doing here?"

"Well, I was just on my way into town to bring Ron a turkey sandwich, and I thought I'd check on you. I brought you some food in case you were hungry too."

She opens up the picnic basket to reveal blackened, stuffed flounder, fresh cornbread served in a hollowed-out gourd, and three different freshly baked pies: pumpkin, blueberry, and apple. I grab her face and gently stroke her cheek with my thumb, wiping away her tears. She presses her head up against the bars.

"Sheila."

"I know, Saint James, I shouldn't have—"

"Stop. Yes, you *should have* brought me all this food." I lean my head against the bars too. "Is that the only reason you came here? To give me a delicious meal that you would never cook for your own husband?"

She shakes her head no. Through her tears she whispers, "I need it. Please."

"You need what, Sheila? I want to hear *you* say it."

"I need that pork sword," she whispers as she points down to my cock. Of course, I know damn well that's what she needs, but it's nice to hear it out loud sometimes. I grab a tin coffee mug and run it against the bars as loud as I can.

"Hey, boss man, can you let the lady in?"

"Is she your wife?" the deputy screams back.

"Nope."

"Then no, she can't come inside your cell. Anything you want to do outside of it is your business."

Sheila and I look at each other, realizing this probably isn't a good idea. So instead, we decide to go with doggy style and forgo any attempt at missionary. She turns and hikes up her dress, pressing her ass into me while gripping the cell bars. This gives her great leverage. After the first few thrusts, I let out a piercing shrill like something out of Greek mythology as I orgasm. Sheila turns and looks at me, confused.

"Oh my God, what just happened?"

"Sorry, it's just, you're the first woman I've been with since I've been in jail. You get it, right?"

She pushes her dress back down and turns to kiss me. "Of course. I'm so sorry. I didn't know I was the first. You've been in here almost half a day."

"Don't fucking tell anybody about this. Come back in a few days, and we can have a longer sesh, all right?"

She kisses my forehead and leaves. I'm so famished that I immediately start grabbing food out of the picnic basket and stuffing it into my face. The fat Mexican is staring at the food like a homeless man's dog. After mouthing to himself practice sentences of what he is going to say, he musters up the courage to ask if he can have some.

"Do you think I can have your leftovers?"

"Not a fucking prayer, my man. I can still smell you. Keep sewing."

"Please, I'm so hungry."

"Tell you what. If you can go the entire week without taking a shit until I go to trial, maybe I'll give you some food, okay?"

"Okay."

"Look, I'm really fucking full right now and I just need a nap, so I'm going to need you to shut the fuck up for the rest of the day."

The second I close my eyes and drift off I hear the deputy scream out, "Saint James! You have another visitor!"

I look up and see the batshit gypsy woman from the funeral. She's also carrying a large picnic basket on one arm, while staring at me as if she's known me for years. Oddly, she suddenly begins weeping too. I put my hand through the bars and stroke her cheek, exactly the same way I did with Sheila.

"Are you crying because of the smell?" I ask.

"No. My tears are from seeing you confined to this cell. I over-heard your wife explaining to your kids why you were in prison when I was hiding outside of your window today."

"I'm sorry, did you say you were outside *my home*?"

"It was an accident. I dozed off in the bushes while I watched your kids sleep last night. Here, I brought you some pies and some freshly made authentic burritos hand-rolled in Mexico."

"Thanks, but I'm super-full. Just throw those out in the street. I don't have any use for them."

The fat Mexican starts breathing heavily, trying to suck his tears back into his mouth while biting his lower lip like a baby. He bashes his head into the wall over and over again as I rest my forehead against the gypsy's through the cell door. I look deep into her eyes, still trying to place who the fuck she is.

"By the way, who are you? Are you friends with my wife?"

"Never met her. Truthfully, I'm just a gypsy who travels from town to town, reading obituaries and attending funerals. Usually I fuck the husband, brother, or father of the deceased. Occasionally I'll hang around outside their house for a few days afterward; that way I feel like I really know them."

"Why?"

"I get off on it. It's like I have my own secret throughout the day."

"That's pure fucking insanity. Look, I appreciate the food and whatnot, but the deputy won't let you in because you're not my wife."

"That's cool. I just wanted to take you in my mouth through the bars."

"Someone has already been *there* earlier," I say as I point down to my crotch.

To my chagrin, this somehow makes her even more into it. Never one to disappoint, I unzip my pants, and she begins to fellate me through the bars. Whoever this gypsy woman is, she's a fucking pro. After about twenty minutes of her working me over like a mime pulling rope, I explode in her mouth. Upon completion, she puts her index finger up to her lips and begins peeing all over the floor. When she finishes, she slaps me across the face and leaves without saying a word. Exhausted and depleted, I walk over and collapse on my bed. Just as my eyes close again I hear the deputy yell out, "Street James, you have a visitor!"

"Jesus Christ! Who is it?"

When I look up, I see Louretta standing there, holding yet another picnic basket. "Oh my God, you look like hell. I didn't know it was going to be this bad in here."

"Please kill me! Just fucking kill me!" the Mexican screams, as he tries to cut his wrists open with a butter knife. Realizing it's too dull, he throws it to the ground and takes off running headfirst into the wall, knocking himself unconscious. I shrug my shoulders at Louretta.

"This is what I've been dealing with in here for the last twelve hours."

"Am I standing in urine? It smells like urine."

"Yeah, let me get you out of that. Boss man, this is my wife. Come let her in."

The deputy takes his sweet-ass time walking back to my cell to open the door. He pulls a giant key ring off his belt and fumbles through what looks like a thousand skeleton keys before selecting one and opening the door. When Louretta enters, he slams the door behind her.

"One hour with the missus, Saint James," he says as he leaves.

We walk over to the bed and I put my head in her lap. She runs her fingers through my hair and stares deeply into my eyes with a sad look on her face. I know what this look means, because I've seen it 4,203 times.

"Do you want me to make love to you? I know you've been in here a while."

"That's really sweet, Lou, but honestly, I just want you to lay with me and hold me right now."

This is the first and last time I have ever said those words to a woman in my entire life. Dead serious. After doing back-to-back loads, I'd really be struggling to keep the clothesline up and I just want to get some sleep. She lies down next to me and puts her head on my chest. I can feel her tears soaking through my shirt as I close my eyes.

She whispers to me sweetly, "It *really* fucking stinks in here."

"I know. Next time you come, can you bring a sewing kit with more string? It's a long story." Before she can answer, I fall fast asleep.

An hour later, the deputy politely wakes us up by banging all his keys against the cell bars. As Louretta gets up to leave, I grab her ass with a strong squeeze, nothing playful about it. She'll definitely masturbate to that ass grab later, trust me. There's nothing like being groped by a full-fledged criminal behind bars to send her home with an itchy middle finger around the panty-line area later.

After hitting the bottle of laudanum, I get maybe another hour of sleep, then the deputy wakes me up yet again. "You have another visitor, Saint James."

Deep in a laudanum haze, I walk over to the cell door. "Who is it?"

"It's *me*. I'm your visitor," he says, standing there.

"What?"

"I want to suck your cock, man."

"What the shit?"

Fully awake now, upon further examination, I realize that this *isn't* the deputy. It's the crazy gypsy woman wearing all of the deputy's clothes, including his oversized boots. She's also wearing what appears to be his shaved-off mustache, which is glued above her upper lip. As she fumbles with the keys to let herself in, I freak out.

"What the fuck are you doing?"

"You can either stick your dick through the bars again, or I'm coming in," she says, still in a deep male voice.

"What happened to the deputy?"

"I knocked him out with chloroform and took his clothes. Have you ever been blown by a deputy?"

"No."

She laughs. "Awesome, then this will be a new experience for both of us, because I've never blown anyone *as* a deputy. Exciting, isn't it?"

"Not really."

"Use that fear and release it into my mouth when you jizz. If you have to hit me afterward, I want you to know I welcome it."

At this point, I am physically afraid for my life and I let her blow me as the deputy. It isn't easy to orgasm, let alone maintain an erection, but I do it. After I cum, she grabs my right hand and decides to smack herself in the face with it. She then looks up at me in shock and walks out, twirling the key ring on her finger.

"Lights out, Saint James!" she yells out to me, still using her deep deputy voice.

This concludes my first full day in jail.

Chapter Ten

WHEN YOU'RE RICH, IT'S OKAY TO MURDER PEOPLE

After a week of sitting in this hellhole, one thing is certain: jail is boring as shit. There is literally nothing to do in here. If it weren't for the bottle of laudanum I stashed and the insane amount of sex I've been having, I probably would have hung myself . . . exactly like the fat Mexican is trying to do in the cell next to me right now. The deputy's keys jangle as he walks up to my cell.

"Your trial is today, Saint James. Put these on." He hands me a set of handcuffs.

"Mustache is coming back in real nice, boss," I say with extreme sarcasm.

"If I ever figure out how you did this . . ."

"You should post a wanted sign up in town."

He bristles as he unlocks my cell after I put the cuffs on. On my way past the fat Mexican's cell, he screams out, "Oh, thank God!" He sprints over to his hole dug in the ground and pulls down his pants as fast as he can. This isn't good.

The noises I hear next can only be described as what I imagine a grown elephant would sound like giving birth to triplets standing upright on an old hardwood floor. The deputy and I look at each other and then run for the front door like two robbers who just threw lit dynamite into a safe. Except this time, we don't make it out quickly enough.

The shit smell catches up with us a few steps before we hit the front door, causing us to vomit upon impact. We hit the ground and prepare for the next wave. With both of us vomiting uncontrollably over and over again now, we are forced to help each other. Through our tears, we make a silent pact not to leave the other one behind.

Do I hate the law? Worse than dysentery, but I wouldn't wish that smell on my worst enemy. I muster as much strength as I have left and carry the deputy outside.

When I kick the front door open, I fall to my knees as I am finally able to inhale clean air again. The thirty marshals that are waiting outside to escort me to the trial immediately draw their guns, thinking I have killed the deputy. That's when the next tsunami wave of raw stink hits their faces, inducing vomiting amongst them as well. One marshal physically can't take it and puts his gun to his head, ending his own life.

"Somebody shut the fucking door!" one of the marshals screams out.

Five or six marshals finally stagger to the front door and shut it. The town doctor will later declare two of them legally blind. Also, the local schoolhouse will be evacuated and closed for the remainder of the day. The last thing I remember is hearing the Mexican's laughter echoing out of his jail cell, as the marshals lead me to the courthouse. That putrid fucking smell will live in our clothes like smoke after you've been standing too close to a campfire.

When they lead me into the courthouse, it is packed, buzzing with anticipation. Louretta and all my kids are seated in the front row of the gallery. Even Daniel is propped up in the corner, still in a full-body cast. Seeing them makes me realize how much I've missed them.

Seated in the row behind them, I see Sheila, who gives me a slight index-finger wave. Next to her is a man licking his lips. Goddamn it, it's the gypsy woman dressed as an old man with a fake long, gray beard. I shake my head and take a seat at the defense table. Directly behind me sits Ron, holding a large sketch pad and a piece of charcoal.

I turn back toward him, as the jury is led in. "Is that for tomorrow's paper?"

"Yes. It will go to print tonight."

"Make sure to shade in my cheekbones to accentuate them if you're using a close-up. If it's a full-body shot, just shade the fuck out of my crotch, obviously."

He nods his head, as a fat judge in his fifties walks in. Immediately shuffling in after him is the prosecutor, also in his fifties. He takes a seat and winks at the marshals, who turn to each other and laugh.

"Good luck, Saint James. No one beats Prosecutor Van Buren," one of them spouts out.

Van Buren? Shit. He's related to the Schlägers. The feds have brought in a ringer to take me down. At this point, though, I have no idea to what extent.

The following is the exact word-for-word transcript from the court reporter of the trial. (Relax, it didn't last long.)

Judge: All rise. (Everybody stands) State of California vs. Saint James Street James, on this day, August 2, 1853. I understand that Mr. Street James is representing himself in this trial?

St. James: I am, Your Honor.

Judge: Do you have any previous legal experience?

St. James: Yes I have, Your Honor. I successfully represented myself in Yermo, CA, in 1845 when I was wrongfully accused of selling teeter-totters to a group of legless children. I also represented myself in Carson, CA, when I was fourteen years old. That time I was wrongfully accused of operating an underground tortoise fight club. Both trials resulted in not-guilty verdicts, Your Honor.

Judge: Were they snapping turtles?

St. James: No sir, Your Honor. They were box turtles injected with chili powder. Allegedly.

Judge: Strange. Prosecutor Clyde Van Buren out of West Virginia. Van Buren? Any relation to former president Martin Van Buren?

Prosecutor: Yes sir, he's my father.

St. James: Hey, he took a shit at my house! What are the chances?

Judge: Quiet, Mr. Street James! Mr. Van Buren, he is a great man. Also, quite an impressive lawyer.

St. James: Objection, Your Honor. I am also a great man and an impressive lawyer too, yet I was not recognized as such when I presented you with the legal trials I have successfully won. I want that on the record.

Judge: Noted. Gentlemen, let's hear your opening remarks. Prosecutor, you have the floor.

Prosecutor: Thank you, Your Honor. Ladies and gentlemen of the jury, this man sitting to my left is a stone-cold murderer. A killer. An assassin. A man so filled with violence and hatred that he murdered seventeen to nineteen brothers in the *same* family. One of them was mentally *and* physically retarded. Can you imagine the grief that the other seventeen brothers will incur when they come out here next week to bury half their family?

St. James: Jesus, how many fucking brothers do they have, man?

Judge: (banging his gavel) It is not your turn to speak, Mr. Street James. Please continue, Mr. Van Buren.

Prosecutor: Thank you, Your Honor. Mr. Street James also murdered two marshals, and caused another one to take his own life. He may have even murdered the new town sheriff, though the body has not been located. I have sequestered over 176 witnesses who saw him kill each and every one of these men. They have all agreed to testify against him. In all my years of being a lawyer, I have never seen a more open-and-shut case than this one. I feel confident that after you hear all the testimony, you will agree with me. (Pointing at the defendant) This man should, and will, be hung in the middle of the street for all the wrong he has done. Thank you, Your Honor.

Judge: Thank you, Mr. Van Buren. Mr. Street James, you may address the jury.

St. James: Did I kill all these people? Probably, but I'm going to deny the shit out of it when the "official" trial gets under way. Even if I did do it, let me ask you this, what kind of family can you kill seventeen to nineteen members of, and it only adds up to *half*?

Judge: (bangs his gavel) Get to the point, Mr. Street James! By the way, what kind of name is "Street James"?

St. James: Topographic, Your Honor. The point is, I have seven kids, so I can appreciate family. . . . Pardon me, I now have only six kids. My other son is dead, because the Schläger brothers dipped him in a scalding pot of melted gold and hung his statue from the top of my barn. Do you know how heavy it was to move just so I could put him in the ground for a proper burial? No one helped me carry him. There was only one set of footprints in the sand that day. (Points to the prosecutor) This fuck didn't say anything about that, did he? No, he just focused on the negative, like an asshole. He stands up here in his bullshit seersucker suit and tells you how many sweet witnesses he has. You know how many witnesses I have from the events that I'm accused of? Three. *Two of whom are dead, killed by the Schlägers.* The last witness is my son who the Schläger brothers shot sixty-three times and who now resides in a body cast over there. (Points to a child in a body cast who is drooling on himself) Am I supposed to apologize for only having one witness who is still alive? I'll call him to the stand if you want. I'll ask him questions for weeks if you want. (Points to the prosecutor) You want to drag this trial out with your witnesses? Fine. I'll drag it out with mine. We can take this bitch into the middle of next year! (The courthouse erupts in applause)

Judge: (banging his gavel) Order! Order in the court! Mr. Street James and Mr. Van Buren, can I see you in my chambers for a brief recess?

St. James: Is there liquor in these chambers you speak of?

Judge: Now! (All three men exit and retire to the judge's chambers)

End of the court transcript

When we walk back into the judge's chambers, I immediately spot a bottle of whiskey and begin to pour myself a glass without asking. The judge unzips his robe, exposing his nude body, including his dong. He sits in a hardback chair behind his desk and lights up a cigar as he wipes the sweat off his brow, exhaling deeply.

"It's hotter than the devil's dick in there."

"I hear that, brother. There's nothing but duck butter inside these old jeans," I say as we have a laugh.

"What is this? What's going on here? Are we going to have a trial or what?" Mr. Van Buren barks out.

"I'd rather not. This really will take forever, and it's August. Let's just see if we can hammer something out."

Mr. Van Buren is outraged. "But he killed twenty-two people, including two marshals and possibly a sheriff!"

"Those boys killed his kid and a couple of clowns who provided nothing but joy to this town. As far as the marshals, he said it was an accident, and I believe him. You said yourself you haven't located the body of the sheriff. So what do we got? Some eye-for-an-eye common-man shit, which isn't worth going to trial for that long. I say we give him a day in jail for each man killed, minus his kid, and a fine."

"Judge, with all due respect, that's only a twenty-one-day sentence," Prosecutor Van Buren thunders.

"With a *fine*," the judge fires back at him.

Time to seal this deal. "Whoopsy," I say, as I cough loudly and throw the remainder of my gold from my leather pouch on the ground.

The judge laughs so hard his dong bounces up off the chair. Mr. Van Buren appears outraged.

"I have never seen anything like this in my career! You will go down eventually, Mr. Street James, I can assure you of that."

Mr. Van Buren slams the door and leaves. After he storms out, the judge and I end up having eight more glasses of whiskey, just rapping about life. He then picks up a tin can connected to a piece of yarn that is hanging out the window behind him.

"You want to share a prostitute?" he asks me.

"I thought you'd never ask."

We laugh mightily, and he yells into the can, "Find me any prostitute off the streets, George!"

"Where does that line go?"

"I have no idea! I don't even know a George."

More laughter ensues, and at this point, I just assume he's drunk. Five minutes later, the ugly prostitute who blew me on the street opens up the window and crawls in. After dusting herself off, she holds up her index finger, before sticking her arm back out and dragging in the piece of plywood with a hole cut in it. The judge roars in delight.

"Glorious!"

Indeed it is. I line up behind him, and we proceed to get properly blown. Twenty minutes later we exit his chambers and walk back into court. The judge bangs his gavel and announces to the court that we have reached a plea deal. Once the plea is read, the entire courtroom erupts in joy and laughter. Women are crying tears of joy, men nod their heads in respect, my kids are jumping in the air, and Daniel continues to drool. The only ones *unhappy* about my plea are the marshals . . . and Louretta. I lean in to kiss her, but she moves her head out of the way.

"What's wrong? I'll be home in three weeks," I say to her.

"Jesus, Saint James, I could hear the judge moaning from his chambers. Everyone could. Do you have to throw it in my face how many women you sleep with when I'm not around? I look like a fool."

"You knew who I was before you married me . . . *a rape survivor.*

Sometimes my past follows me, baby, you know that, but I'm a man first and foremost."

"You're also a *father*. Look at them. Look into the eyes of your children."

I scan down the row of my children, who look up at me with the same desperation in their eyes as when I was late for dinner. Daniel nods off and falls over to the ground, his hard body cast hitting the floor. Louretta holds her tears back as it sets in that maybe I haven't been the best father.

"Come on, children, let's go home. You'll see Daddy in a few weeks." She helps Daniel up, puts him in a wooden wheelchair, and rolls him out of the courtroom with my other kids in tow.

Even though it's the gold rush and it's completely acceptable to sleep with whores, there is an unspoken rule about discretion. Your wife is your wife, whores are fucking whores, and you don't bring that shit inside the home. She knows my sexual prowess is that of an untamed wildebeest, and she's not fucking stupid. Today, I made her look like an asshole, and I genuinely feel bad about that.

As the marshals lead me out of the courtroom in handcuffs, I glance over Ron's shoulder and see that he has gone with a close-up sketch, which is probably the right move. My cheekbones are accentuated exactly how I like them. I nod at him and show him a sliver of respect, so he can at least try to have some semblance of a normal life. Plus, I might need him in the future for something.

On my way back to jail, I notice a slew of wagons rolling into town stocked full of gold-mining supplies and crates stamped with the word "Schläger" on them in big, black letters. One of the wagons stops in front of the saloon, and Manuel walks out to meet it. Prosecutor Van Buren strides over and stuffs a thick envelope of money in his hand, and starts laughing in his face as he makes a throat slash sign. That's when it dawns on me that he isn't in town *just* for the trial; he is in town for something more.

I think back to Van Buren's opening remarks in court when he said that shit about me only killing half of them and that the other half were coming to bury their brothers. He was planting the seed. Sven was right—they don't die, they multiply. A coldness washes over me as I realize that I'm going away for three weeks and can't do anything to stop them from taking over. At least there is a gentlemen's code that you don't harm another man's family while he's locked up.

A solitary tumbleweed kicks up dust, rolling down Main Street as I stand there, lost in thought about how I shamed Louretta. My moment of reflection is soon interrupted as the front door of the jailhouse opens and the remnants of that smell hit me square in the face again. The deputy leads me back to my cell, where I see the fat Mexican up to his old tricks, sitting on the makeshift toilet while eating a can of beans. He looks up, surprised to see me.

"You're back already?"

"Yeah, I'm fucking back, and I'm in here for three more weeks. I know you ripped the seams on your cheeks, and I want you to know a man took his life because of it. Your stink ends right now for the next three weeks, and so help me God, if I hear even a fart come out of you, I will kill you. Got it?"

He begins sweating heavily. "One week was hard enough, I don't think I can hold out for three whole weeks."

The deputy takes the cuffs off me and puts me back in my cell, closing the door behind me. He hands me a sewing kit, and I look at him surprised.

"It's from your wife. She gave it to me in court today, said you asked for it."

I nod my head and squeeze the kit in my hand, feeling worse about my actions earlier today. Goddamn it, Louretta. It's the little things that women know how to get you with.

"Thanks, boss," I say to him.

He nods at me in appreciation for saving his life earlier. "You do what you need to do if his poop chute opens up. I'm indebted to you, and I won't say a word, whatever you decide to do."

The deputy tips his hat to me, acknowledging what I did for him earlier, and I respect him for that. He recognizes I saved his life, and in return, I decide to live out my three weeks in jail without harming him. Plus, if I rub out another member of the law and get arrested for it, how am I going to pay off the judge? I blew all of my last remaining chunks of gold, and my mine shaft is dry. Pun intended.

Chapter Eleven

AN IRONIC NAME FOR A CHAPTER WHEN YOU LOSE ALL YOUR MONEY

When I walk out of jail and into the streets after my three-week stint is over, I look up at the sun and think, "Holy shit, that thing is goddamn bright." I take my shirt off, letting the rays greet my unusually pale frame. A familiar gallop echoes through the air, and of course it is my steed trotting over to greet me with a saddlebag full of dynamite and a fresh bottle of laudanum. I missed this son of a bitch. While I was on the inside, five things became painstakingly evident.

1. My wife *definitely* hates me. She didn't visit me one single time after I was sentenced. No food, no basket-weave HJs. *Nothing*.
2. I'm completely out of gold, and I'm fucking broke. I can't even dig through my family's shit anymore.
3. The Schläger brothers have completely taken over. According to the newspapers I read every day in jail, this is no longer a

backwoods operation, this is some well-run gangster shit. Van Buren is now running shit like a boss. He's in charge of the new set of Schläger brothers that came to town, and they are 100 percent business. They even wear suits and bowler hats now, so they're more easily identifiable.

4. Never trust a gypsy woman. The disguises might have been diversion tactics just so she could have an actual dude blow me, which I think is what she wanted all along. Throughout the three weeks, I became so exhausted from her comings and goings that I couldn't tell if it was really *her* anymore. In fact, I'm almost positive that on one of my last days in the clink, I was fellated by a normal dude named Bobby. I can't be too sure, but this is my best guess. She finally has the best secret of all time to keep to herself.

5. The human body can only go eight to ten days without having a bowel movement before you die. That fat Mexican didn't make it out of that cell. I'm not sure if the coroner took out the stitching or not before they buried him, but my guess is no. The bowels of hell would have opened and swallowed the earth. Rest in—actually, fuck that guy.

Riding up to my house, I see Louretta and the kids planting fruits and vegetables in a brand-new garden, something that we haven't had since we were poor. The kids all scream and run up to hug me as I hop down from my horse. I'm genuinely grateful to see them.

"Hold your hands out; I brought you guys back something from the joint."

They clap excitedly as I pull out a set of chess pieces that I have hand-carved out of soap. My youngest sticks a bishop into his mouth and starts violently sneezing. Louretta walks over and pulls it out from under his tongue. He laughs and walks away.

"He's walking now? Wow, I really missed a lot these last three weeks."

"He's been walking for two years," she says hastily.

"Oh, he's *that* one. Got it. What's with the garden?"

"We're out of money. It's been up to me to feed and raise six kids while you were locked up getting blowjobs from strangers for the last month."

"What? Who told you that?"

"There's all of these rumors going around town that strange women *and men* have been crawling in and out of your cell at all hours of the day."

"Well, that's why they're called *rumors*, because there's no room *or* circumstance for matters of the blindness of others' chatter—"

"Just stop. Do you even hear yourself? You're just making up words. Look, I don't have it in me to fight with you. Dinner is almost ready. Wash up before you come inside the house. You smell like a fart in water."

I smell myself as she walks into the house. Indeed, I do stink. Daniel walks out of the front door using only one crutch now. He pulls a bottle of laudanum out of his back pocket and tosses it to me. I catch it and immediately begin double-fisting with the other bottle my steed brought me. Daniel pulls his shirt up over his nose as he hobbles down the front steps of the house.

"I love you, Dad, but you smell like a dead seal's cock."

We walk down to the river so we can catch up while I wash myself. In the water Daniel regales me with stories that in no way, shape, or form happened. It becomes painfully clear that he has been hallucinating on laudanum for weeks. On the way back, a bald eagle swoops down in front of us and Daniel punches it in the face, knocking it dead to the ground. I stare at him in wonderment.

"Did you just punch a bald eagle out of the air?"

"Yeah. It's the only way we can eat meat around here now," he says with a shrug.

"What do you mean?"

"You'll see."

He tucks the bald eagle into his back pocket and hobbles back up the steps of the house. I take a seat at the kitchen table with my boys, and lead them in a "We want food!" chant as we bang our forks and knives on the table. It was nice to be home . . . until Louretta walks over with bowls of salad, placing them down in front of us one by one.

"Um, what the fuck is this?" I ask as I throw my utensils down in disgust.

"It's *salad*."

"I know what it is, but where is some form of meat?"

"We can only afford to eat what we grow off the land, so we have to eat salads. We can't afford any chicken or livestock, hence no meat is served."

"Daniel just punched a live bald eagle out of the air, cook that up. Give your mom the bald eagle." Daniel pulls it out of his pocket and slams it down on the table.

Louretta's face grows red with anger. "If you guys want to punch bald eagles down out of the sky, then cook them yourself!"

"What the fuck is that supposed to mean?"

"It means that I still believe in this country, and I don't condone killing the animal that is the symbol for American freedom just so we can have some meat! I wasn't raised that way!"

"You were raised by a bunch of ginger bushes who sucked the starch out of every last potato they came across in Ireland. It wasn't until this little leprechaun married you and gave you a magic pot of gold so that you could have all this shit!"

"Where is that gold now, huh? Oh, right, it's melted onto our dead son who was murdered because of you!"

"I could have fucking knocked a gold chip off his shoulder, but you—"

"Don't you dare say it!"

I think better of it and shake my head. She stares me down before storming up to the bedroom with her salad as I sit in silence. My boys look up at me expectantly. I know I have to do something.

"All right, who wants to go outside with me and build a campfire to cook up some bald eagle?" Everyone immediately raises their hands except Daniel, who stares off into the distance mumbling.

"Dad, I killed a leprechaun while you were gone. I never told Mom. It's in the barn."

I shake my head and rub my temples. "I'm sure you did, buddy. Let's go start that fire."

That night, my six remaining sons and I build a campfire and enjoy some fine bald eagle, fresh out of the sky. Daniel keeps the beak and hangs it on a necklace with a collection of other beaks, from other kills he's made. I really did miss a lot while I was gone.

After putting the kids to bed, I head out to the barn to think. It's nice to curl up with my steed again and not have to listen to Louretta cry. If you think hearing a woman cry is terrible, try hearing her cry in an Irish accent. Holy shit, it's awful. With the barn door open, and my head resting on my steed's belly, I stare up at the bright full moon with sadness.

As delicious as it was, that tiny slice of bald eagle tonight isn't going to fill me up on the reg. I'm not eating salads every day, and we can't keep eating bald eagles. Actually, maybe we can. Judging by Daniel's necklace, this isn't the first time he's done this. Why am I considering this? I need money ASAP, so I start to ponder all my options.

First of all, the Schläger brothers have too much manpower. Can I overtake them and kill them all again like I did the last seventeen? Probably, but they'd more than likely kill my entire family in the process. Is that something I'm willing to risk? I take another sip of laudanum to silence these thoughts.

That night I toss and turn in constant fear that the gypsy woman is going to try and wake me up with a blowie. I finally give up on sleep as the sun slowly begins to rise. Strapping the saddle to my steed, I notice a foul smell drifting into my horse's stall. I draw my gun and cautiously walk back to check the rest of the stalls. When I approach the last one, the smell gets stronger. I kick open the stall door and see a dead leprechaun lying faceup on the hay. Holy shit, that son of a bitch actually did it.

"Daniel, come outside and bury that leprechaun you killed! He fucking stinks!"

"Okay, Dad!"

I hop up on my steed and we ride into town, but this time I am not looking for a drink and a whore to start off the day; I'm looking for a job. As I gallop through the town, I see Schläger brothers everywhere. There are at least two of them dressed in their suits and bowler hats in almost every store along Main Street.

The Schläger name is on every marquee outside as well: Schläger Bros. Mining Supplies, Schläger Bros. Fine Suits, Schläger Bros. Furniture, Schläger Bros. Wigs Shoppe. You name it, they own it.

Two Schläger brothers suddenly drop a crate they are carrying, and it explodes right in front of us. I pull the reins on my steed abruptly, as hundreds of doorknobs roll into the street. Their immediate laughter makes it evident that this was done on purpose. I dismount and draw my guns, kicking a doorknob back toward them as I cock my pistols.

"Does this mean you want me to open you up? I'll put a doorknob straight up your fucking ass and keep turning."

"Break it up, boys!" screams the deputy, who has become the sheriff. His mustache has fully grown back. He runs out into the street and blasts a street howitzer into the air, just as the Schlägers start going for their guns. In the process he trips over a doorknob and falls backward on his ass. His shotgun accidentally discharges again, and he shoots the leg of one of the Schläger brothers clean off his body. Mr. Van Buren flies out from one of the shops as the legless

Schläger brother rolls around on the ground in agony, holding his stump. He picks up the leg and points it at me.

"What in the hell is going on?" Van Buren forcefully asks.

The sheriff stands up. "I'm sorry Mr. Van Buren, I was trying to break up a fight when I slipped on a doorknob and blew off Jared's leg by accident."

I don't even try and contain my laughter as I say, "On the plus side, you might be able to put it on one of your homemade tables in your furniture store."

"Goddamn it, Sheriff, we hired you to protect this town, not to turn people into sack-race contestants," Van Buren says as he throws the leg down in disgust.

"Wait, *you* hired the sheriff?" I ask. "What is it that you're actually doing here in town, Mr. Van Buren?"

"Same as you, I'm a businessman. I heard through the grapevine that this was a good prospector's town."

"You wouldn't have heard that from a former president, would you?" I ask. "You know, I wasn't kidding when I said your father used our outhouse."

"Oh, I'm well aware. *Your* father had sex with my mother in it. That heinous act tore our family apart for years."

My jaw hits the dirt. Maybe my dad was cooler than I thought. Not cool enough to warrant a longer first chapter, obviously, but good on him. At least I know where I get it from. I stare at Mr. Van Buren inquisitively.

"So you're pissed because my dad fucked your mom and you came here for revenge? Now we're getting down to brass tacks."

"She was a first lady!"

"Yeah, but was she a *lady first*? Wink."

The sheriff quickly looks away, and Van Buren tries to compose himself. "Look, Saint James, we don't want any more feuding between you and the Schlägers. You noticed no one came after your family while you were locked up, right? We're running clean businesses now, and we don't want any shenanigans. Here's a few dollars for your trouble today." He walks over and hands me twenty dollars. "Sorry about the doorknobs."

"The shiny ones on the ground or the ones wearing the bowler hats?" I ask as I take the money.

"Too good, Mr. Street James. Too good," Van Buren says before forcing a fake laugh. "Let me get these doorknobs out of your way so that you may safely travel through."

He motions for the brother with both his legs still intact to pick up the doorknobs. I feel like killing this motherfucker right here and now for giving me a shitty fake laugh, but killing a president's son would bring down the fury. Now that I know why he's *really* here, I need to fucking strategize. I tip my hat and reholster my pistols, hopping back on my steed. Oh, and that bullshit I said about not starting off my day with a drink and a whore so I can look for a job is obviously out the fucking window now. I can read the want ads at the whorehouse while getting blown and enjoying a whiskey thanks to this newfound jack. Time to mosey on down to the saloon.

Just walking in and smelling the prostitution reminds me how much I miss it. When I cozy up to the bar, I notice row after row of Goldschläger bottles stocked on the shelves. There's no other bottle of any other kind of liquor in sight. It's *all* Goldschläger. Looking around at the few patrons scattered about, all I see are gold flakes in everyone's glasses, and they're *all* drinking it. I whistle Manuel over.

"You hiding the good shit from these dirtbags? Give me a whiskey, Manuel."

"I can't, Street. The Schläger brothers bought my bar, and their liquor is all I'm allowed to serve."

"Why did you sell it to them?"

"I didn't really have much of a choice. Van Buren and the sheriff made me sign it over on account of me being an Indian and all. They said I could still work here and that they wouldn't kill me as long as I tell people I'm Mexican."

"Well, we've already taken almost all your land in this country, so this shouldn't be too much of a shock, I guess. Sorry, Manny. I tell you what, bring me a glass of that shit to whatever bedroom I walk into back there. I don't want any of them to see me drinking that unicorn piss in public."

Manuel nods as I pick out a whore and walk back into an open bedroom. I pull my pants down and sit down on an old rocking chair inside the room, before reading the paper. The whore I chose is one of my regulars, a sweet-natured girl named Claire who knows not to start straddling me immediately.

"Do you want me to go down on you?" she politely asks.

"No, I just want to sit in this chair and let my junk air out for a bit while I read. Why don't you take off your clothes and crochet on the bed for a few?"

She strips and pulls a set of crochet hooks out of a nightstand drawer next to the bed while I scan the want ads. The only people hiring are the Schläger brothers and their various businesses. The local Wagon Wash is hiring, but there's no way I'm cleaning huge chunks of horseshit off people's wagons.

Manuel walks in with my glass of liquor and puts it on the table next to me. When he sees what's happening, he tries to leave quickly, but I don't let him. I enjoy making people feel awkward and pretending I don't know that it's awkward for them. Maybe I do have a little gypsy in me.

"Manuel, do the Schläger brothers own every single business in this town now?"

"Almost. The only one they don't own is that empty lot next to them Chinamen."

"What place is that?" I ask as I fold my paper and tuck it underneath my scrotum.

"You know, the place next to where they feed dead people to their pigs to get rid of bodies for people who don't want to pay for funerals?"

"*Love* that place. They serve exquisite squirrel dick there on sticks while you watch the bodies being eaten."

"Yeah, I wouldn't know about that. I saw your Chinaman over there working the other day as I passed him on the way in. He lost a couple more teeth."

"That happens when they're made of mud. Perhaps I'll stop by and pay him a visit. By the way, do you want to watch me screw?"

"You have to pay extra for that now. I need the cash."

"You want me to pay, so I can teach *you* a lesson in fucking? Get the hell out of here."

Manuel still doesn't make eye contact as he leaves, so I pull the paper out from between my legs and throw it at him as he walks away. I glance over at the bed, where Claire is putting the finishing touches on a pair of mittens for me; the kind with the rounded ends, not the ones with fingers. From under the bed, she pulls out a fully knitted pajama onesie with a barn door for the front and the back. It's monogrammed with the initials SJSJ on the front, right over the heart. I can tell she wants my approval.

"That looks like shit. What man would sleep in a onesie? Burn it and use the hand covers as queef mittens."

"What's a queef mitten?"

"Pretty self-explanatory. It's a mitten you queef into. I'm gonna go; I'm pretty turned off by the baby gifts you made me."

Claire starts to get emotional when I walk out, so I purposefully leave the door open so she can watch me walk *directly* into another whore's bedroom next door. I throw a one down on the end table and begin having sex with the new whore in the other room against the wall, knowing full goddamn well Claire can hear us. As I bang away, louder and louder, Claire screams, "Please come back, Saint James! I'm so sorry!"

"Nope!"

Claire goes ballistic and starts slamming her hands on the wall that I'm banging against. I punch a hole through it, so she can see my face as I climax with the strength of a thousand zebras. That will hopefully teach her never to knit baby clothes for a grown man again. I stick my face through the wall, into her room, and scream at her. "You made me do this! I'm not a fucking baby! Also, the climate out here doesn't ever call for clothing like that!"

I thrust in a hard final set of ten, letting her know that I came *a lot*. When I finally finish, I cup my hands like I'm wearing mittens and double-wave her good-bye, before pulling up my jeans and leaving.

On the way out I hear Manny call out to me, "You're going to have to pay for that hole in the wall."

I throw a one-dollar bill over my shoulder at him and leave. After that animalistic sex, I have a hankering for squirrel dick. Plus, it would be nice to see my Chinaman again. Not because I've missed him, but mostly because he is probably still poorer than me, and I need a pick-me-up in the old self-esteem department right about now. Rounding the corner of the saloon, I immediately hear the sounds of wild pigs ripping through the flesh of a dead body, while a few Chinamen laugh. I tap one of them on the shoulder.

"Who is that being eaten?"

"A schoolteacher," one of the Chinamen replies with laughter.

The Chinese are hard-core and don't give a fuck. If someone dies, they chuck the body and keep on working. It's business first, and I respect that. A frail man fights his way through the small crowd that has gathered to watch the schoolteacher get devoured. He's got twenty squirrel di tied to an old broomstick.* I hold my hand up, indicating I want five squirrel di.

---

* "Di" is the proper plural when describing five or more squirrel dicks.

As the man gets closer, I see that it's my Chinaman. I fucking told you, they just keep working no matter what happens. He grins from ear to ear, and I can see there are only a couple of cones left in that ice-cream shop that he calls a mouth. He goes in for the one-armed hug, which I obviously avoid to keep my street cred. Plus, homeboy is fucking filthy.

"Good to see you, sir," he says with the type of enthusiasm people that poor should never have.

"Isn't it? How is the squirrel di industry?"

"Can't complain. Just trying to save up enough money to fix up my father's boat to go back to China and get the rest of my family."

"Why's that?"

"I heard they need people to build wailwoads. Sorry, most my teef are gone."

"You should probably just say train tracks. Never mind. More important, your dad had a boat?"

"Yeah, how do you think we got here?"

"I'm gonna be honest, I thought you just prayed really hard, then magically showed up. You guys have a mystical culture."

"Indeed we do. How are things with you?"

"A kid died, got dipped in gold. I killed a couple dozen people, went to jail, and became poor. It's been a weird month."

"So sorry to hear about that," he says with genuine concern.

"Thanks. I've been getting through it all right, thanks to this shit." I pull a half-empty bottle of laudanum out of my back pocket and take a pull.

"Oh, that made of opium. My people invented it; there is tons of it over there."

"What do you mean?"

"Let me buy you some squirrel di, and I'll explain."

Normally, I would never eat with the help, but his laugh is genuine, something I haven't heard for a while, and so I decide to break my own rules. We walk for the next hour or so, sharing squirrel di as I pretend to care about what he talks about, which for me is a lot. Usually I don't even bother to pretend at all. The Chinese are really into their families and shit, so I'm sure he is talking about them a lot. As we walk to the edge of town and along the river, he points to a small dock, and I see his boat.

It looks like shit now, but you can tell it might have been sweet at some point. He shows me how much work has to be done, pointing out the trouble-spot areas, which are every two feet of the boat. There's also an enormous amount of dried blood on the main deck. I don't even bother to ask him whose blood it is, but he tells me anyway.

"That is my father's blood. A swordfish jumped up in the boat and speared him in the heart a couple times."

"A *couple* times?"

"The swordfish jumped *twice*."

"Same one, huh? It must have really wanted to kill him."

He nods his head yes, then stares out into the distance with enormous pride. I let him have this moment before asking him where I can take a shit. The squirrel di are running through me like a Class 5 rapid in the Rio Grande right about now. It's probably because they have so much protein in it. Those little squirrel di are totally worth a small amount of ass discomfort.

My Chinaman leads me into a bathroom on the boat, below deck. Sitting on the wooden makeshift toilet, I notice that the interior of the boat is in pretty good shape. To relieve my butthole pain, I grab the bottle of laudanum out of my jeans, which are now around my ankles. The rest of my money that Van Buren gave me falls out when I remove the bottle. I notice my bottle is dwindling fast, and I need more. Doctors roamed from town to town back then, or else I would have robbed that motherfucker by now. My eyes rapidly shift focus to the money on the floor and back to the bottle. Oh. My. God.

My Chinaman's words begin playing over and over in my mind: "My people invented it . . . there is tons of it over there." That's when the lantern goes on. I need to start a drug cartel! Without wiping, I quickly pull up my pants and race up to the deck.

"If I help you fix up this boat and go to China with you to get your people, could they get me a shitload of opium?"

"We gonna need a bigger boat. We have fields of it!"

I'm so fucking happy I *almost* hug him. Obviously, I don't. Instead, I extend my hand and offer it to him to shake like he is a fellow white man. Also, for the first time since I've known him, I finally decide to ask him, "By the way, what's your name?"

Tears start to well up in his eyes. I can tell he's been waiting for a long time for me to ask this. He regains his composure and says, "Samantha Davis."

I pause for a moment, thinking I have heard him wrong. "I'm sorry, could you repeat that?"

"Samantha Davis. When my father first came over to America to see if it would be safe for us, he snuck onto a barge and locked himself inside the first suitcase he could find. The name tag said Samantha Davis on it. Those were the first words of English my father could pronounce when he sailed over, so this name was very special to him."

I smile back at him. "How about I call you Sam for short?"

"Why?"

"Because that's what friends do, we give each other nicknames. Today we have become true friends . . . but you'll still work for me."

Chapter Twelve

WHEN ONE DOOR CLOSES, ANOTHER PERSON IS PROBABLY FUCKING BEHIND IT

Riding back to the house at night, I have a new sense of hope. Van Buren thinks he can ruin my life? Good fucking luck. Louretta, unfortunately, does not share the same enthusiasm when I tell her I am going to sail to China to go get opium with a man who's legal name is Samantha Davis. To say she goes ballistic would be an understatement.

"What are me and the children going to do for money while you're off in China for God knows how long?"

"Look, I'll probably only be gone a month, a year at the longest. I haven't really figured out their calendar yet. It's all fucking animals, so who knows? Here's sixteen dollars; this should cover everything while I'm gone."

She slaps me hard across the face, but I don't move one single inch. Instead, I raise my hand and gently pull her face into mine.

"Lou, I have to provide for this family. You said it before—I'm the fucking man, and I have to figure it out. This is me figuring it out. I need you to trust me."

"I don't know if I can do this all by myself without you. The three weeks you were in jail were hard enough. Now you want me to go a whole month?"

"It's probably leaning more toward the year side, but yes, you'll be fine. Look, I married you because you were a strong, unyielding woman. I know you'll run this house stern but fair while I'm gone."

I kiss her mouth hole like I might never see her again. On my way out, I leave the rest of the money that Van Buren gave me on the kitchen table. Like I said before, sometimes a man has to do what the fuck a man has to do. Also sometimes a man has to do whatever the fuck it takes to provide. Becoming a drug lord just feels right.

Outside, I see a light shining down in the front yard, coming from the upstairs window. I look up and see the silhouette of Daniel leaned up against his crutch, smoking a cigarette. He nods at me with a "you're doing the right thing" look on his face. I reach into my back pocket, grab the bottle of laudanum, and throw it up to him.

"This is for you, son. For the hard times."

He catches the bottle and stares at the remaining contents, both of us not sure when we're going to see each other again. After about ten minutes, I finally say to him, "I'm going to need you to take a swig of that bottle and throw it back down. That's the last of my stash, and I'll probably need it."

He quickly takes a sip and throws the bottle back down to me. In the window next to Daniel's, I see Louretta gazing out at me, crying. I tip my hat to her and hop up on my steed. Resigned to the fact that I need to do this, she nods her head and quietly closes the curtains.

I ride hard and reach Samantha Davis's boat just after midnight, and wouldn't you know it, that motherfucker is *still* working on it. He looks up from the deck and waves at me as I arrive. When I come aboard, he hands me a block of wood with sandpaper wrapped around it and asks me to join him in sanding the deck. I wave him off and start laughing.

"No fucking way, Sam. It's after midnight. I'm going to hit the sack, then try and catch a little shut-eye. Don't even think about waking me till about nooner, got it?"

"Of course. Sorry."

"It's okay. I'm going to take the captain's quarters, obviously," I say as I walk down the steps to retire below.

Surprisingly, there's a decent-sized bed in there. As I light my lantern (so I can watch myself jack off), I think about how many Asians were probably crammed into this very bed on their journey over. I wonder if they were afraid. I wonder if they had hopes and dreams on the long sail over to my country, just as I will have hopes and dreams on my way over to theirs. Mostly, I wonder if they were all women and what they looked like. With my pants pulled down, I reflect on this before drifting off to sleep to the sounds of wood being sanded. Double entendre and pun intended *again*.

For the next three weeks, we work on the boat day and night. Actually, I take the noon to 1 PM shift, while Sam works the rest of the day. I hate to admit it, but we are a great team. As a token of my appreciation, I carve him a set of wooden dentures out of a couple of the dried, bloody boards we remove from the deck that his father died on. Even though my wood-whittling skills are terrible, anything is better than what he has left in his mouth. It will be worth hearing him talk with a lisp for the remainder of the trip.

Once the boat is finished and deemed ready to sail, the only thing left to do is name it. Naming a boat is the most important thing. Sailors have often said that a good boat name will get you through rough seas if you're about to face certain death. It's not something to be taken lightly, so I decide to name the boat after Sam's father, and paint the word "*Twice*" on the back. I still can't believe that swordfish had the tenacity to jump again. Samantha weeps as I christen the boat by smashing the now-empty bottle of laudanum against the bow. The goddamn boat turned out pretty amazing.

Finally ready to sail, I put it on wheels, tie it to my steed, and head west for the Pacific Ocean with my new best friend, Samantha Davis. He instructs me to ride to San Francisco, which apparently his people are docking in and out of as an entry point into this country. He says we'll be able to get a small crew of FOBs to work with us as cheap labor on the back-and-forth.

"What's an FOB?"

"Fresh Off Boat."

I laugh, not knowing how super candid he is about racism until this point. This camaraderie will help us on the long journey we are about to embark on.

My steed halts as we hit the shoreline of the Pacific Ocean sometime around early evening the next night. As the sun is going down, Samantha and I stare at the crisp blue water in silence, taking in its beauty. I have never seen the Pacific Ocean before, even though I've lived just a little more than a hundred miles from it most of my life. It is majestic. It also looks exactly like the Atlantic Ocean, I will later find out. What a fucking sham.

As we unhook the boat and push it out into the water, my steed stares at me as if to say, "Take me with you. I love Asian horses." But this isn't his journey, it is mine. Plus, this boat isn't Noah's fucking ark, and I don't know how he'd survive, although I do give it a fair amount of thought. Instead, I whisper into his ear, "Go home and look after the kids. Take Daniel on a dynamite montage."

He reluctantly nods at me, and I hug him around the neck like he is my firstborn. I really don't know what the fuck I am getting into out here, or if I will survive, so I want him to know I love him. Our embrace is broken up by the sounds of Samantha whistling loudly, followed by a handful of cheers from Chinamen walking out of sand bunkers they have hand-dug into the beach (which, as it turns out, they are sleeping in).

As they walk aboard the boat, I slap my steed on the ass, signaling him to take off. Confident he is going to be fine, I walk aboard the boat and immediately rip off my shirt to show that I'm in control. A handful of Chinamen, led by Samantha, push the boat off the sandbar, out into the water. I salute them as they climb aboard, and demand they raise the sails.

"Due west, men!"

"Is there another way?" Samantha asks.

"You will not address the captain like that." I slap him hard across the face. "Grab a fucking mop!"

He smiles and immediately starts cleaning the decks. He knows it's important for me to show the men who's in charge on the first day. I don't care how skilled these dudes are at sailing a boat across the Pacific, I'll be goddamned if I'm going to take orders from someone, especially someone of a different race. This is 18-fucking-53.

The next several weeks sailing over to China go relatively smoothly. That is, if you count vomiting between your legs as you shit simultaneously on a toilet every twenty minutes as "smoothly." If I'm being real, I can't recall much of the trip after day three, when the scurvy set in. The last thing I *do* remember is foaming at the mouth as the Chinamen held me down and cut my arm open with a knife to release the tainted oxygen from my bloodstream.

The next thing I know, I wake up with a lime stuffed in my mouth and another one stuffed in my anus as Samantha stands over me shouting, "Welcome to China!"

"We're here already?" I ask half-dazed.

"*Already?* You've been in bed for three months."

After removing the limes, I slowly get up out of bed and stumble over to grab a bucket of water to splash on my face. My arm is still throbbing. I look down and see a dirty rag covered in dried blood wrapped around the wound. As I run water over my face with my hands, I feel a sweet-ass lumberjack beard.

I look at a small mirror that is hanging on the wall, and I barely recognize the man staring back at me. Not only do I have a huge beard, but my hair has grown past my shoulders, and some of it is tied in Viking braids. Who the fuck braided my hair while I was bedridden with a horrible disease? It is weird, yet somehow matriarchal.

I will say this: I'm pulling off this look with ease, almost as if I was born from a long line of seamen. You knew that line was coming, so you're welcome.

When I walk up the steps to the bow of the boat and look out at this gloriously strange land they call China, my first thought is how beautiful it is. My second thought is, "Holy shit, there are a lot of people here." Thousands upon thousands of Chinese people are working in rice paddies and fishing for food, all of them with a precise discipline. Probably because they know they'll be hungry an hour later.

Stepping off the boat, I am immediately greeted by hundreds of them. Most of them are staring at me in awe, while they touch me. I look over at Samantha, puzzled.

"What's happening?"

"They have never seen an American before," he says with a lisp and slight laughter.

"How do I say 'Ladies touch first' in Chinese?" I ask.

"女士們第一次觸摸."

"Oh, cool," I respond.

I repeat his exact phrase back to the crowd that has gathered, and only the women start grabbing me.*

Samantha lets the gorgeous women take me away, while he runs back to his village to get his people. He is compassionate about the long boat ride over with a bunch of dudes and understands that I

---

* From then on, I was perfectly fluent in Chinese. I felt confident that this was the only phrase I needed to learn, and I turned out to be right.

need to have sex with a woman. Or multiple at the same time, what-ever they're cool with over here. Spoiler alert, it turns out to be mul-tiple. I scream out to Samantha to come find me whenever he gets his shit together. After what I am about to experience that night, I don't care if he ever finds me. It is obvious I am destined to be here.

The Asian women lift me off my feet and carry me high above their heads six miles into the town of Quan Po. Sorry, I just made that up. I can't remember the name of the town. Point to any city on a map off the eastern coast of China and pretend I'm there; every-thing in Asia looks the same.

As we enter the main street that goes through the center of town, people come out of their shops and businesses to view me. They are clapping, hurling fresh fish at me to eat, and offering me karate les-sons. Strangely, they're all dressed like former president George Wash-ington. Asia really has always been way behind the fashion trends.

When we reach the top of the street, I notice a wooden house with steam rising from it. A painted large sign hangs underneath the faded red bamboo roof shingles. I see the letters "女士們第一次觸摸."

"What does that mean?" I ask.

One of the women responds, "Ladies touch first."

I told you that is the only phrase I need to know. A large wooden door opens, and I am hit in the face by a burst of hot steam. The women slowly lower me to my feet. As the steam dissipates, even hotter Asian women greet me, ones who haven't been working out in dirty rice paddies all day. They are all wearing beautiful silk kimonos and wooden sandals. Suddenly, I realize I'm in some sort of exotic Asian bathhouse.

I have heard rumors over the years that these are traditional in the Far East, but I never believed it. When the women take off their kimonos and start undressing me, I know that it's real. They pick up buckets stuffed with loofah sponges and walk me back toward a gigantic bath. Four more nude women greet me once I hit the edge of the water. They spin me around, cross my arms, and slowly baptize me in the warm water like I am baby Jesus.

There is something truly special about Asian women. They're like exotic angels, wise beyond their years, who barely speak and always clean. They really know how to take care of a man, all the while possessing a high level of tolerance for shit, much more so than American women. This night I experience their hospitality first-hand, beyond your typical bukkake session.

When I emerge from the water, I feel like I have been reborn. Mostly because one of the women is scrubbing my penis a little too hard with the loofah, and it feels like I am being circumcised again. Another woman puts a pillow on the edge of the bath and lays my head back, sticking a long hose connected to a hookah in my mouth.

She smiles sweetly and asks, "Opium?"

"What? You can smoke this shit too?"

She nods her head yes, and I roar with delight. I'm going to be rich as fuck when I get back to America.

Fully relaxed, I hit the hose and inhale deeply. Holy. Fucking. Shit. On impact I am instantly flying. This isn't the genie in a bottle I've been sipping on back in 'Merica. This shit is as clean as Zeus's dick. My eyes roll back in my head and stay there until I cough them back forward, releasing the smoke from my lungs.

To top it off, there are six different women simultaneously scrubbing every limb and orifice I have. One of them begins to ride me slowly, and although you know my stance on sex in the bathtub, this time it's different. It's more sensual somehow. Probably because I'm high as shit and I don't have to care about my performance. They're the ones who gave me drugs, so whether I last two minutes or an hour, they knew what they were getting into by sticking that hookah in my mouth.

One by one, each woman takes turns riding me like the tourist burros at the Grand Canyon. I make love to what must be thirty or forty women for what seems like an eternity. When I'm finally ready to orgasm, they all line up in the water and stare directly into my eyes. There's something really special about forty beautiful Asian women waiting for you to erupt. It's a heightened sensation, like sniffing glue on the roof of a stranger's house.

After achieving the climax of the century, I unleash double Dutch–style ropes across everyone's faces and chests. Yes, *all forty women.* Immediately upon my finishing, two girls grab my arms and pull me up out of the large community bathtub. They proceed to wipe me down with warm towels that feel like they have been resting above a fireplace for hours.

Shortly thereafter, I am led down a long, narrow hallway, where another door magically opens. Thousands of rare Chinese butter-flies fly out of the room and down the hall. A myriad of silk pillows cover every inch of the floor. Nude women are sprawled everywhere around another hookah in the center of the room that resembles a Chinese Medusa, with multiple hoses flowing out in every direction.

Each of them takes turns smoking and passing the hoses toward one another. There is none of that junkie eagerness to them, probably because they know it's endless.

When a hose gets passed to me, I take a deep pull, and one of the women starts pouring hot oil all over my chest. One by one she walks around and pours oil all over everyone. Free of all inhibitions, we begin rolling around on top of each other mindlessly.

Technically, what transpires over the next several hours would be classified as "sex," but to call it that would cheapen it. It is a full-blown bacchanalia, or high-grade orgy to you common folk, and I am the only man involved. I can't even guess how many orgasms are had. Women ride me, they ride each other, and a couple of them even fuck a hand-carved anatomically correct wooden statue of Buddha that rests in the corner of the room.

There is no sexual judgment over here; you are free to do anything. *Anything.* For instance, during the second hour of this fuck-fest, I start crying. Not like a bitch, or in an "I miss my home" way, but actual weeping, like a mature man reaching the highest sexual peak he's ever known.

Imagine Christopher Columbus dipping his balls in American soil for the first time. That's the type of crying I'm talking about. The unabashed feeling of reaching a new plateau and wondering if you will ever achieve something like that again. I empty my entire soul into the room, and just when I have nothing left, the women pick me up and gently carry me out.

"I don't think I can take anymore. I have no more energy," I say, defeated.

AT NIGHT SHE CRIES, WHILE HE RIDES HIS STEED

They giggle and lead me through yet another door, where I'm hit with more steam. As the steam retreats, an entirely different type of oasis appears in front of me. A beautiful nude chef stands behind a hibachi grill cooking fresh shrimp, steak, chicken, and fried rice. She smiles and flips a cooked shrimp at me from across the room, and I catch it in my mouth. It is the tastiest little shrimp I've ever eaten. The girls lead me to a seat in front of the grill and pour me a glass of rice wine. They know a man doesn't like to be bothered while he's eating, so they leave.

It's the first peaceful dinner I've had in a long time. After the chef finishes cooking, she draws a smiley face on the grill in oil and then lights it on fire. I can't help but applaud. Afterward, she leads me back to the opium den, where we drink some more wine and smoke while I am massaged again until I fall asleep. When I awaken eighteen hours later, we do the exact same thing all over again. I am addicted—not only to opium, but also to this new way of life. The only question that remains is, how long will this last? How many days can one man experience sexual utopia? Turn the fucking page, and you'll have your answer.

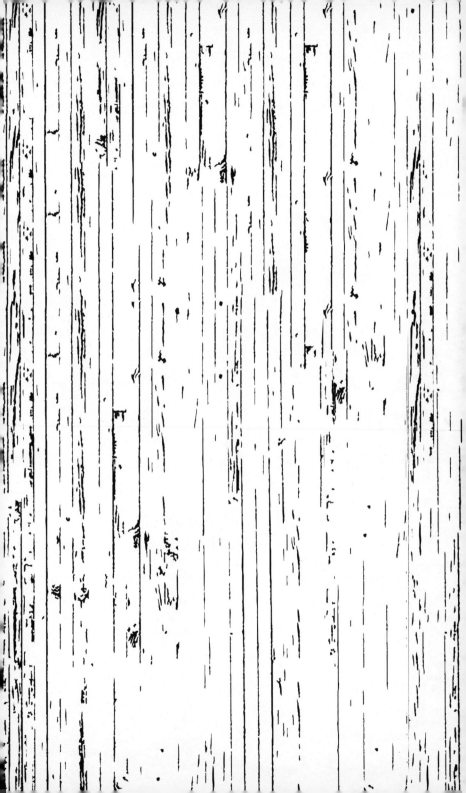

Chapter Thirteen

AFTER SIX YEARS, I AM FINALLY READY TO LEAVE CHINA

It turns out six years is pretty much the max amount of time you can live in utopia and have endless orgies every day. Who knew? Also, eating grilled hibachi food every day, which is delicious and something I used to consider to be entirely possible, has ended up taking its toll on me in the form of a ridiculous sodium intake. In layman's terms, I have been ingesting more salt than a humpback whale. My blood pressure is so high that I have lost all feeling in my extremities.

I try to soldier through, but when one of my baby toes falls off and it takes me nine days to notice, something has to give. Once I lose my sexual abilities, the women have no use for me. They are kind enough to make me a wheelchair out of bamboo and wheel me into town so I can meet up with Samantha Davis again . . . if he's even still here.

I flag down a man who is running up the street towing a rickshaw behind him. The man stops and smiles at me with big wooden teeth stained with dried blood. Son of a bitch, it's him. That's such a Samantha thing to do. His ability to find a job anywhere is truly remarkable. We share a chuckle and he tells me that his family is all loaded up on the boat, ready to go.

When I ask him if they've been on the boat for the last six years waiting for me and he says yes, I feel a tad selfish for what I've done. That guilt goes away pretty quickly when I look back at the skyline and see the bathhouse in the distance, and think about all the sex I had there. I will miss this land.

Since I can't feel my legs from all the sodium, Sam lifts me into his rickshaw and runs us toward the boat, into the Chinese sunset. Watching him run at top speed makes me incredibly thirsty, so I pull off the canteen that is bouncing up and down around Sam's neck and drink all of its contents.

"Did you and your family gather up the opium I requested?"

"Yes, boss. They even fully processed it for you, so we could fit more in."

"Excellent. Remind me to double your pay when I open up my new business back in America."

"So I'll get two cents a day?"

"I guess. You drive a hard bargain."

Upon arriving at the dock, I'm almost positive that I suffer a small stroke brought on by attempting to climb the rope ladder to board the boat. After I place my swollen left foot into the second rung, a shooting pain runs down my right arm, I smell burnt hair, and I black out. To be fair, I smell burnt hair the rest of the boat ride back to America, because that's how Samantha's relatives cut their own hair—by lighting a match, then blowing and hoping for the best.

Much like on the journey over here, I don't remember much about the journey home. I vaguely recall Sam's relatives nursing me back to health with the opium. That shit really does cure any ailment you have. Also, at some point during my sleep, I think someone shaves my face and all my pubic hair off, which is apparently an old Asian tradition. It wards off sickness from recurring. Or Sam's uncle shaved it and glued it to his face to fill in his own patchy beard. Either way, I'm grateful. If he wants to have a pube beard, so be it. He's his own man.

Three months pass before we approach US soil, and I miraculously feel better than ever. My sexual confidence is sky-high. I stand at the bow of the boat and take in this "new" America. A lot has changed in six years. San Francisco seems more prosperous, bustling with people. There are also a lot of dudes in fishnet stockings, which seems strange, but years later will make perfect sense.

I am happy to be back in the States, but I'm missing something between my legs. My steed. Even though it has been a while, I haven't lost any stank on my sweet two-finger whistle when I summon him. Everyone stops what they are doing as the whistle echoes throughout the land. I cup my ear and wait patiently, knowing that beautiful son of a bitch will come running.

Moments later, far off in the distance, I hear his hooves galloping across the amber waves of grain and through the purple mountain majesties—before finally appearing in an all-out sprint down toward the docks. Watching his long strides, all I can think of is how this motherfucker symbolizes everything powerful and free about America.

As he trots toward me, I step down from the bow of the boat and greet him with a long embrace. My pistols hang in their holsters around his neck. God, it feels good to holster up again. It also feels good to stick someone up and steal their carriages, so my sixty-person Asian crew can ride back into town.

As they line up and cram themselves inside, I realize that twenty or thirty of them are women I've slept with at the bathhouse over the years. We share knowing glances, and a few of them even graze my cock out of respect.

Asians are just a step above slaves during this point in America, so we get a few looks from people on the ride back to my house. Someone even screams out, "What are you, yellow?" I refuse to answer, because I can't tell if they are just being observational.

Truthfully, I'm not concerned about what people think. After being in their country and experiencing their culture, I realize that these people are the future. If I want to have a successful business in America, I need workers that I can pay virtually nothing, preying on the fact that they are just happy to be here.

When our carriages come up over the countryside toward my casa, I feel a twinge of nervousness in my stomach. After all, I haven't seen my family in six years. I'd be lying if I said I didn't think about them all this time. For instance, I remember this one time when I was all like, "You know it would be really nice to have someone to speak English with," and they came to mind.

As we draw closer, I see my six kids doing chores out in front of the house. Physically, they are almost unrecognizable now, because they have all grown into little men. Daniel, who is now visibly older, smiles at me warmly, then spits out a huge stream of tobacco juice.

I halt my steed at the edge of the garden, which has grown tremendously. An abundance of fresh fruits and vegetables now populates the garden. When I hop down, my kids race over to greet me. My youngest son, Bourbon, actually asks who I am. At least they can all speak and understand orders now.

"Hey boys, I brought you back something from the Orient."

"Samurai swords?" Bourbon screams in excitement.

"No, something better."

When I pull off my cowboy hat to reveal six sets of Chinese finger traps made out of bamboo shoots, they seem a little let down. Each of them grabs one, and they jam their fingers into them as they run off . . . except Daniel. He just glares at me as he strokes the sides of what appears to be a mustache, then he casually picks up the last remaining finger trap out of my hat.

He shakes his head in disappointment. "What the fuck am I going to do with this, Dad? Put my dick in it?" he says in a deeper register. Holy shit, he's *really* grown up.

"It would probably fit, you son of a bitch! You got any milk to go with those cookie crumbs above your lip?" We share a laugh, and I punch him in the gooch as I put my hat back on. He doubles over on the ground and holds his crotch, trying to catch his breath.

"Welcome home, Pa."

Louretta comes running out of the house screaming, "What's all the commotion?"

She stops cold in her tracks as our eyes fuck. Staring at her, all I can think is, "Wow, she's gotten older. I was afraid this would happen." Don't get me wrong, she still looks good, but once that wagon goes downhill, you know that thing is going to need a lot of repairs after it crashes. Her tits are still huge, though, so I take my hat off again out of appreciation.

"Good to see you, Lou. You look almost as good as one can at your age."

"Where have you been? It's been six years, Saint James."

"Has it? Shit, I'm sorry. I knocked over my abacus and lost track of where my beads were. Anyway, I'm home now."

"Thanks, I see that. Who are all these people?"

"*These people?* Come on, that's pretty racist. How about we discuss this over a nice hot bath that you draw for me? Oh, and if you want to say 'Welcome home,' you can do that too."

"Welcome home," she says flatly. I do, however, notice a twinge of relief in her eyes when she says this. Another little boy runs out of the house who I don't recognize at all.

"Welcome home, Pa," he says.

I stare blankly at him, before motioning to Louretta. "Who the fuck is this?"

"Your new son. Remember the night Totally Fucking Mexico died?"

"I knew I got you pregnant! I'm the fucking best."

She shakes her head and turns to walk inside, as my new son runs out to pet my steed. I grab Daniel and pull him aside. "Help the Chinamen unload the bricks of opium I brought back and stack them in the barn. Smoke a little if you want to test the merch. I'm gonna go have sex with your mother and try to smooth everything over."

"Cool," he says as he walks over to greet the Asians.

Louretta seems annoyed as I read the newspaper while she fills up the tub. Sensing she's nervous about being intimate, I take it upon myself to break the ice. When she goes to retrieve the last couple buckets of water, I use my newspaper and some tub water to create a massive Russian nesting doll out of papier-mâché over my penis. She tries to play it off like she's not amused when she comes back in.

"What is that, Saint James?"

"Sshhhhhhh. Watch."

One by one, I pull off thirty individual dolls, before revealing my huge erection underneath. Louretta finally cracks a smile and begins to take off her clothes. It's time to go to pound town.

As she undresses, it dawns on me that this is the first time I haven't bathed with thirty to forty women at the same time in six years. Even though Asian women are great, they lack in the breast department, which is something I sorely missed. I don't know who said life is all about the small things, but they're fucking liars. Nothing beats a good old-fashioned set of white woman's breasts heaving like a fat man jogging.

Never one to window shop, I get up from the tub and make out with Louretta, slamming her hard against the wall. We crash completely through it, falling down onto Bourbon's bedroom floor, never breaking penetration. I glance over and see his hobbyhorse rocking back and forth from the force of our landing.

"Are you thinking what I'm thinking?" I whisper.

"That we shouldn't be doing this in one of the kids' rooms?"

"Nope. I'm thinking we should turn that hobbyhorse into a *professional* horse."

"What's a professional horse?"

"One that lets you fuck on it."

I lift her up and carry her over to the horse and sit down, with her facing me on my lap. With subtle precision, I begin to rock back and forth, gripping the handles on the horse to keep a smooth and constant motion. As we make love over the course of the next two hours, I occasionally look out the window and see the Asians unloading the opium into the barn with Daniel. Also, a few of the Asian chicks I have been banging over the past six years have gathered outside and are staring at me. The whole thing is very erotic, and I find myself looking directly at them as I climax, just as I did in China.

Louretta holds me like a conversation, squeezing my biceps hard, her nail marks leaving fresh trails of blood. She is no doubt thinking about the new sexual agility I have acquired over the last six years. The air is so thick with the scent of sex and blood that I have to open a window after I finally pull out.

"Daniel, when you're done loading that opium into the barn, could you come up here and fix the wall I crashed through with your mom?"

"Why is it *still* me?"

"Because I'm still your fucking dad! Thanks!"

He shrugs his shoulders and throws down a brick of opium in disgust. I flip him off, double-birding him as I shut the window. Louretta stares at me with a bewildered look on her face, probably because I'm still hard.

"So what's your grand plan now that you have all of this opium? What are you going to do with it?"

"Smoke it. I'm also going into business with it. Do you have any of that money I gave you six years ago?"

"Yeah, a couple dollars left, I guess. Why?"

"Good. I'm gonna need it. I'm going into town tomorrow."

Louretta follows me as I walk back into our bedroom through the giant hole in the wall. After putting on my jeans, I reach into my pocket gingerly, because this fucking boner still hasn't gone down. I pat my other pocket and that's when it hits me, "I almost forgot, I brought something back for you."

"Should I close my eyes?" Louretta asks eagerly.

"No, I want you to see it."

Carefully, I begin to pull a beautiful full-length silk kimono out of my jeans pocket. Seeing the happiness in her eyes when I hand it to her, I think back to Curly when he pulled that card out of his chest as he was dying. He probably wanted the same reaction I just received. Oh well, know your audience, I guess. Louretta puts on the kimono and walks over to the window.

"How long are they going to be here?"

"If all goes well, they should be gone by tomorrow afternoon. A few months tops, maybe four years at the most."

"*What?*"

"Relax, they're all self-sufficient, and I've obviously instructed them never to come inside our house. Plus, I bet they could help you out with that bullshit starter-kit garden you got out there."

"That garden fed us for the entire six years you were gone!"

"And I commend you for it. You're a good woman, and I'm gonna feed your mouth forever with what I'm about to do . . . but Daddy had a long journey, and I need some form of meat. I'm sure Daniel has some bald eagles stashed away. Prepare me some dinner; I gotta go check on my Chinamen." I kiss her on the cheek and walk out.

Later on at night I sit down and eat a home-cooked bald-eagle dinner with my family. My boys have outgrown their whiny bitch stage and they aren't crying or shitting in cloth diapers anymore; instead they have manners and respect. Even the new one is cool, whatever the fuck his name is. I meant what I said earlier about my wife being a good woman. It doesn't mean I'm not going to cheat on her every chance I get; I'm obviously still a man, and she knows that, but I have a newfound respect for her as I stare at her across the table.

"You've done a great job with these boys the last six years, Lou. Raising these little fucks without me must have been hard."

She seems genuinely touched by this. "Thank you. Do you want to help me put them to bed after dinner?"

"Not really. But I'll do a walk-by after they're down and fire a couple invisible six-shooters their way as I pass. I'm going to go have a cigarette on the porch."

Daniel perks up. "Can I come too, Dad?"

"You sure that little brush above your lip won't catch fire? Kidding. Come on out, son."

A full moon lights up the Coloma sky on this beautiful night as the two of us share a smoke and catch up. "I actually missed this place," I thought, as I look out at the grave site where I fucked a stranger on top of my dead kid's casket. There are a lot of great memories here.

"So what's been going on the last six years?"

"Just partying and bullshitting. The usual. I lost my virginity a few weeks back," Daniel says nonchalantly.

"Did you pay for it?"

"No, it was my teacher at the schoolhouse."

"I bet your grades improved."

"All As. Ma has never been prouder."

I pat him on the knee. "That's great. That's really fucking great. How's the town?"

"The town is good. It's really changed, you'd hardly recognize it. The Schläger brothers run everything now. People dress up when they go to town. All the men wear suits and the women wear these big, poofy dresses."

"Get the fuck out of here."

"There's even a mayor now. There was an election and everything."

"Who's the mayor?"

"Mr. Van Buren."

"Of course. I'm sure *that* was an honest election. That bastard is going to love me being back. How's your shooting, by the way?"

"I'm the best there is. Been practicing every day since you left."

"All right, tough nuts, we'll see. You want to come into town with me tomorrow?"

"Hell yeah! I even got my own steed now."

"What? Where did you get a horse?"

"It was the strangest thing. Mr. Paulson brought it over and left him when he was a foal. He seemed angry about it. It wasn't too long after you left."

I cough up smoke and laugh. Holy shit, I had forgotten that I let my steed fuck his gimpy horse. Classic Saint James. This father-son moment is perfect, until I see Samantha's uncle shitting inside our drinking bucket. He waves at me and flashes a big, toothless smile. Most of his pube beard is still intact. I wave back at him and lean over to Daniel.

"Clean out that drinking bucket when he's done shitting, okay?"

Daniel rolls his eyes as I walk into the house and upstairs to do the walk-by of my boys sleeping. The first two look so peaceful in their beds that checking on the rest of them seems unnecessarily boring. Instead, I blow out my lantern and dip into my bed, putting my arm around Louretta, whispering sweetly into her ear, "Let's bone in the morning before I leave. Love you."

The following morning we do bone indeed, before I head out with Daniel into town. It's strange riding alongside him all grown up on his own horse. Luckily, his horse got my horse's genes, and it's a pretty decent steed.

Trotting down the main road into town, I'm truly taken aback by how much it has changed. Daniel wasn't bullshitting. The buildings are bigger, and the makeshift Schläger Brothers signs on every storefront are now professionally hand-carved, neatly hung above the shops. The population has almost doubled in size, and everyone is dressed to the nines. All the men are wearing tailored suits, while the women wear dresses with corsets. Daniel and I look like a couple Mexican strawberry pickers compared to everyone else. People start ogling and pointing at us like we are the goddamn help.

For the first time in my life I feel like a lower-class citizen. Not one woman stares at my cock. Why? Because women don't stare at a poor man's cock. They know they can fuck a poor man anytime, but a rich man, you have to stare at his cock and let him know you're there.

I might as well have ridden into town with the crotch cut out of my jeans, because these women don't even glance below my belt. If you ask me, that's the *real* poverty line. With my anger boiling, I instruct Daniel to quicken the pace so we can get to the deed office faster.

Once we make it in safely, I am amazed by how much this place has changed as well. It is a real bank inside, and the stink is gone. People are actually conducting business in here, instead of bartering for shit. Meanwhile, I'm standing here with two wadded-up dollars in my hand, looking like a beet farmer who has taken his mildly retarded son into the big city for the first time. Someone even hands Daniel a nickel on the way out like he is Tiny Fucking Tim.

After about twenty awkward minutes of our standing here feeling out of place, a nebbish teller with glasses comes over and walks us over to his desk. He motions for us to have a seat and checks his watch, as if we are taking up his precious time. Daniel nudges me, annoyed.

"Dad, why don't you just blow a hole through the roof like the old days and tell everyone to fuck off?"

"First of all, there are two armed Schlägers working security at the exit. Second, I need to keep a low profile until I'm able to open up shop. You understand me?"

"Yeah, I guess so."

"Do you want some bread, son?" the teller asks Daniel with pity.

"What the fuck? No, he doesn't want any *bread*. We're here for business. I'm Saint James Street James!"

"I know who you are. You used to run this town back in the day. The only reason I even brought you over is out of respect for who you once *were*."

Infuriated, I lean down to Daniel and say, "Remember when I said I was going to keep a low profile earlier? That just went right out the fucking window."

I pull out my guns and twirl them swiftly before laying them down on the desk, pointed directly at the teller. Daniel taps his pistols as the two Schlägers go for their guns. I smile calmly through clenched teeth and remind the teller who the fuck *I once was*.

"Since you already know who I am, I'm surprised you don't remember that I'm the fucking stone-cold killer who will not hesitate to rip out your eye and skull fuck you in front of all your coworkers. I'll rape your mind so hard they'll be able to hear what you were thinking at age nine."

He stares at me in shock, and quickly tries to backtrack. "I'm sorry, I'm so—"

"Let's also not forget your place in the world versus mine, shall we? You may be able to buy a fancy suit, but you'll never be able to buy courage or a set of dick and balls like these."

In one swift move, I grab his hand off the desk, stand up, and jam it down the front of my jeans. His hand is holding my entire dick and balls. The whole place gasps in horror, and the Schlägers rush over toward me. Daniel rises up and draws his guns with lightning-fast skills, aiming them at both their heads. He really is fast as shit, and they back off.

"What do you feel down there?" I ask the teller in front of everyone.

"I don't know. A man?" he says.

"A man with *what*?"

"A man with a real set of dick and balls?"

"That's right, I'm a man with a real set of dick and balls! Don't anyone fucking forget it!"

Looking each and every person in the eye, I pull his hand out of my jeans and slam it back down on the desk. The teller quickly wipes it off on his slacks and adjusts his glasses, which have fogged up with moisture from his tears. I throw a handkerchief directly into his chest and motion for him to clean his shit up. Realizing the situation isn't going to escalate, the Schläger brothers back off and Daniel stands down. The teller tries to regain his composure.

"What can I do for you today, sir?" he asks.

"I need to buy some property in town. Something I can build a business on."

"Oh, I'm afraid everything in town has been bought up by the Schläger brothers and Mayor Van Buren."

He reaches into his desk and pulls out a new map containing all the property lines. I rip the monocle attached to his coat clean off, and examine the map for myself. This bastard isn't lying; they really have bought up everything in town. Every inch of the downtown grid and all the mines have been purchased by the Schlägers, except for one plot of land with a big pig head drawn next to it. I smile to myself, remembering what Manny told me years ago. I press my index finger down on it.

"What is this? Why is there no name next to this property?"

"You don't want this property. Matter of fact, no one wants this property."

"Why's that?" Daniel asks.

"This is the property next to those filthy Chinamen who feed dead people to pigs when they can't afford funerals. It's disgusting. They do serve exquisite squirrel di though."

I flash a grin at him and ask, "How much is it?"

"Um, it's two whole dollars, sir," he says, like I probably can't afford it.

I pull the two dollars out of my pocket and throw them in his face. "Sold. Draw up the fucking deed."

"You can't be serious. Why do you want *this* property?"

"Do you want to feel my dick again while I explain to you why, or are you going to draw up the deed?"

"I'll draw up the deed."

"Smart man."

I pick my guns up off his desk and put them back in my holsters. Out of the corner of my eye, I notice Mayor Van Buren walk in and casually greet the townspeople milling about. As much as he pretends that he's just popping in to say hello to everyone, I know he's here to see what I'm up to. He politely tips his hat toward me as he walks over.

"Mr. Street James, good to see you back around these parts," he says, smug as fuck.

"It's good to have my parts back around here again."

"What brings you in today?"

"Spell the word 'deed' backward, and that's what the fuck I'm doing here."

He nods sarcastically and then pulls out his own monocle, examining the grid. Jesus, everyone has a fucking monocle now. The teller points to the property I'm purchasing, and Mayor Van Buren raises an eyebrow curiously. He shakes his head incredulously and puts his monocle away.

"Are you crazy buying that property? It's directly next to the Chinamen who feed dead poor people to their pigs. They do have the best squirrel di in town, but what on earth do you hope to do with that property?"

"To build an outhouse and fuck your mom in it . . . or I'm going to open a business there. Haven't decided yet."

"Pray tell, what kind of business?"

"Leisure," I say as I stand up and light a cigarette, exhaling it in his face. "I'll see you soon."

I grab the deed from the teller and walk out. Daniel also gets up and smiles in his face. I can feel Van Buren eye-fucking me as we stroll out. I'm not going to give him the satisfaction of "the look back" over the shoulder. Instead, I keep going and cop a feel of a tit off an unsuspecting woman walking in. Saint James Street James is back, motherfucker.

Chapter Fourteen

DRUGS ARE FUCKING AWESOME, AND EVERYONE WANTS THEM

Over the course of the next two months, the Chinamen work in split crews of thirty apiece. While one crew is setting up rice paddies on my never-ending estate so they can feed themselves, the other thirty work under a veil of secrecy constructing my new business next to the pig shack. They cut down trees from my property and turn them into building supplies and melt down copper they find to make nails. I have so many people working in unison that my hard costs are nothing.

Curiosity begins to spread amongst the townspeople as to what kind of establishment I'm building, and I never say a goddamn word, which only creates more interest. I'll give you a hint, it rhymes with "schmopian schmen." Since the Schläger brothers have shut down my ability to mine gold, it's time to become a hard-core drug dealer.

There are only a couple ways to be rich in my time: gold and drugs. Even being a doctor or a lawyer is more of a novelty or hobby.

Don't even think about being a dentist. If you can tie a piece of string to the back of a doorknob, congrats, you're a fucking dentist.

Operating opium dens is 100 percent legal now. There's nothing anyone can do about it. For the Chinamen's hard work, I agree that they can all live in the den once they are finished. I also agree to give them a cut of the profits for running the place. Don't worry, it is something like 1 percent. Again, these people are just grateful to live and work here, so I am basically doing *them* a favor.

As the building progresses in town, life on the home front has been surprisingly pleasant. Louretta is happy with the new additions to her garden, the kids are all learning karate, and I have been having sex with most of the girls that I brought back from overseas out in the paddies. It is probably one of the most joyful times I have experienced as a married man. It is like being Mormon but with way hotter women, and my wife doesn't know. Actually, it is nothing like being Mormon; I'm just committing adultery again.

As the summer goes on, I see various Schläger brothers spying on me from high above in the hills. Normally, I would kill them and think nothing of it. This time, however, I want them to be curious about my every move. I also want them to see me having sex with these women in the fields, partly for business, but mostly because I'm into that shit. I enjoy an audience, and I like to be watched—big fucking deal.

So I wait, and let them watch me fuck the entire summer. Just as the season is about to turn to autumn, Samantha and his boys ride up over the hill in a carriage behind my steed with huge smiles on their faces. I see a glint in Samantha's wooden teeth that I haven't seen before, or maybe a termite chewed a little piece out; either way, I know that it is time.

"It's ready, boss," he says enthusiastically.

"Son of a bitch! Man, this feels good. I'm so proud of us that I want to throw a party tonight, which you'll obviously set up. Why don't you guys make me some of that rice wine so I can get insanely drunk?"

"We'd love to! You deserve it after how hard we've worked all these months!"

"Tell me about it. My leadership skills are better than I give myself credit for. Now go get a jump on that wine, okay? Daddy needs to get his beak wet."

Then they scurry off. I can tell they are excited, because they actually show a different emotion than "frozen by fear." As I walk through the rice paddies with the sun setting behind me, a cool breeze picks up, sending tingles down my body, probably indicating change or some form of STD. I shiver a little bit but refuse to put a shirt on. A young woman, Soon Lee, who I've been balling for close to a year, maybe longer (they really all do look alike), peeks her head out of the paddies and politely waves at me.

"Mr. Street James, can we talk?" she asks shyly.

"Yeah, I guess. You're kind of ruining this sunset for me, but go ahead."

"I'm so sorry. I just wanted to tell you that . . . I'm pregnant." She then steps out from behind the paddies, revealing her huge stomach, indicating that she's very late into her third trimester. It actually looks like she could give birth any second.

"I know you're pregnant. I've known for *days*."

"You are the father."

"I figured. I never pull out."

"Will you be there for me and our baby?"

I smile warmly at her and answer, "Probably not. I'm not even really here for my own children with my *real* wife, so you're more than likely going to have to ride solo on this effort."

"Is there at least a chance? I will wait for you."

"Maybe someday soon—"

"That's so nice to hear."

"No, you didn't let me finish. Maybe someday, Soon Lee, you will meet another man who will care for you and the child. I'm just not him. You're a special flower that deserves to be watered on. I gotta go. We cool?"

"Yes," she says as she nods her head and bows to me.

"Also, could you grab that wheelbarrow full of broken rocks and discard them about a mile down the river? Thanks a bunch."

As her nine-months-pregnant body struggles to lift the heavy wheelbarrow, I notice a couple more Schläger brothers on top of the hill, spying on me in the distance. Since we're opening tomorrow, I decide now would be the perfect time to test the opium out on potential customers. I hop on my steed and ride in from behind, surprising them with my pistols drawn. They damn near shit themselves going for their own guns.

"Don't do that, boys; I already have the jump on you. If I had wanted you dead, I would have killed you by now."

"Well, what the hell do you want, then?" one of them asks.

"To bury the hatchet. Let bygones be bygones. You killed my son, I killed half your family, but that doesn't mean we can't be friends. How about a little herbal peace offering?"

I pull a long Chinese pipe and a box of matches out of my pants. They look at me suspiciously as they examine the pipe. It's obvious they haven't seen anything like this before. One of them even sniffs the contents of the bowl.

"What is this, some of that crazy enjun shit?" he asks.

"You mean peyote?"

"Yeah, peyote. That shit made me wrap my entire body in leather, cut out only a mouth hole to breathe, and jump off the roof of my house. I landed pecker-head down in my wife's cactus."

"That actually sounds like a blast, but no, the stuff I got here has been shipped in from the Orient. It's a new drug called opium, and it's the smoothest high you'll ever have. No hallucinations, and it *makes* you want to have sex even if you don't."

"That's bullshit. I never heard of it," the other Schläger says.

"It's brand new to the States. I'm opening up a whole new whorehouse in town tomorrow that will exclusively sell it. You sure I can't interest you in a toke?"

They both confer with each other, then smile at me. "You smoke some first to prove that it's safe," one of them says.

"You don't have to twist my dick to smoke this shit."

I strike a match off the bottom of my boot and light the bowl. Through the flame I can see them eyeing me cautiously as I inhale deeply and blow out huge smoke rings. I then pass the pipe to them. Not wanting to be pussies, they each take a hit and try to hold it longer than I did. When they finally exhale, they immediately break into fits of laughter. I pat them each on the back as they continue to smoke. With each puff, they become more entranced in the opium haze. One of them wiggles his fingers in front of his face.

"Man, I feel amazing, and you're right, I *do* want to have sex. Matter of fact, I might go stick my dick in that hollowed-out tree knot over there." He points to a large oak tree down by my house.

"Uh, dude, I got kids and shit. You can totally fuck a tree on the way back to your place if you want, though. Have a good night." I turn and hop back up on my steed to ride off, when one of them calls out, "Hey . . . do you got any more of that shit?"

I smile to myself before turning around. "I sure do. Stop by my grand opening in town tomorrow. Invite your brothers if you want."

"Okay, but what time *specifically* do you open? Because I will be there at whatever time that is."

"Noon. See you gentlemen tomorrow." I tip my hat and ride off not saying another word, knowing that they are already hooked.

After dinner when Louretta is putting down the last of our children, I stop to have a cigarette with Daniel in his room. I wait outside his door until he is finished jacking off. He's fourteen now, so that's pretty much all he does all day. Like father, like son. Speaking of which, my father never let me borrow his socks after the age of ten, a trait that I've taken to heart as well. I knock on the door to make sure it is safe.

"Um, come in, I'm not doing anything," Daniel says hurriedly.

"It's your old man, just wondering if you want to have a cigarette?"

I ask as I carefully open the door. "You look out of breath; should I come back?"

"No, it's okay, I was just doing push-ups."

"Well, it is important to work on your core, but remember to always properly warm up before any exercise. Warming up reduces the risk of injury."

He looks up at me puzzled. "Um, okay. Thanks, Dad."

"I'm fucking with you! I know you were jacking off! You think I give a shit about warming up before exercising? Let's have a smoke, bro!"

I burst out laughing and punch him in the gooch before sitting down at the foot of the bed next to him. We hand-roll a couple heaters and open up the window in his room. Outside I see hundreds of tiny lanterns lit for the celebration this evening. For the first time ever, the Chinese aren't working. Instead they mingle around the barn, smoking cigarettes and drinking rice wine. Daniel joins me at the window.

"It's beautiful, isn't it, Dad?"

"That sounded gay, but you probably knew that the second it came out of your mouth, right?"

"Yeah, that was stupid. I'm sorry. Can I come to the party tonight?"

With the sounds of female laughter trickling through the night air becoming more frequent, I can see the eagerness in his eyes. I lean over and put my arm on his shoulder.

"Not a fucking prayer, my man. Your mother would kill me. But you can watch from your window, and I'll pretend you are sleeping."

"Okay," he says, disappointed. As I turn to walk out and leave, he stops me and asks, "What's going to happen out there tonight?"

"One can never be sure. I just hope I don't wake up covered in someone else's blood in a bathtub full of doll parts. Goodnight buddy."

I walk out with his lantern and quietly close the door behind me. As soon as I turn around, I run smack-tits into Louretta. Both of our lanterns collide and hit the floor, burning down the entire house with all of us in it. Everyone perishes, and there are no survivors. Just kidding. I wanted to make sure you're still paying attention.

Louretta looks up at me, surprised. "Is he asleep?"

"Fast as shit. I thought he was dead in there for a second."

"Good. That makes all of them. Are you going to the party?"

"I thought I'd stop by for a drink. I want to tell them they've done a great job with everything, but I still want them to know I'm their boss. Why, do you want to go?"

"I don't know, I could have a tin cup full of wine and let my hair down."

"If you fucking cheat on me, I'll kill you!" I say angrily.

"What? No, I just—"

"I'm messing with you. You could never find a man as good as me. After you, Mrs. Street James." She smiles and takes my arm, allowing me to escort her out into the rice paddies.

Daniel was right, it is beautiful seeing all the Chinese lanterns lit up and strung throughout the garden. I obviously don't say that out loud, though. As we walk arm in arm, Samantha comes running up with two cups of wine. Half of his wooden teeth are now missing, so I can confirm that termites have obviously infested the rest of his mouth. He seems really happy at the moment, and I don't want to ruin that by pointing out his teeth.

"We did it, boss," he says with a more defined lisp.

"Yes, I did. Big day tomorrow. You excited to finally be able to sleep indoors?"

"Oh, yes, my people have always dreamed of sleeping inside of the place they work all day long."

"I can imagine."

"Are you guys coming out to the barn for the *special* party?"

"Oh, I don't know, Sam."

Louretta nudges me. "Come on, Saint James, it might be fun."

"Lou, people are going to be smoking opium and wearing animal masks. Shit might get wild."

"I'll try it. I should at least know the kind of business you're getting into."

I look at Sam and shrug my shoulders. "Okay, give her the pipe," I tell him.

Samantha smiles and pulls a pipe out of his back pocket. By the way, Chinese people carry pipes on them at all times, which is just fucking classy.

Samantha loads her up a bowl, and I instruct Lou to hold it in as I light it. She's a woman, so obviously she chokes on it and coughs out all the smoke like she's dying. Her eyes start to water and her cheeks get red, then suddenly she bursts out laughing. I take a toke of my own, and we pass it around several times before walking over to the barn.

Samantha flings open the barn doors, and a giant plume of steam hits us in the face. I close my eyes and take it all in, inhaling deeply. Memories of my first night in China come flooding back. I know exactly what the fuck is going down in here.

Once inside, I see they've set up a makeshift bathhouse with people washing each other and having sex inside all the giant horse troughs from the stables. I'm initially surprised at how much water they have taken out of the river. Then I remember they are Chinese. Never doubt their fucking efficiency and attention to detail. The only thing different from the Orient is that this time, there are men in there as well.

I don't know if you've ever seen a penis on a Chinaman, but it's like looking for an acorn in a pile of autumn leaves. When you first see one, there's a lot of algebra involved. You start calculating length times width minus body size. It's hard to tell if their dicks are that tiny, or if they just grow insane amounts of pubic hair? Truthfully, that's a question for the scholars. Louretta gasps and covers her mouth.

"Are you okay?" I ask.

"Yeah, I just never expected that *this* went on. They seemed like such friendly people."

"To be fair, they're all still *really* friendly, but even I didn't know four people could 69 at the same time. It's pretty fucking rad, but if you want, we can leave."

"No. I want to stay. You only live once, right?"

"I hope that phrase never catches on. Since we are going in, we should have a safe word."

Before I can tell her my safe word is "harder," two beautiful nude Asian women grab her and lead us to a trough. They take our clothes off and put us into a makeshift "bath." Once we are seated, they immediately pour hot water all over us. Everyone is smoking opium, and pipes are being passed from trough to trough. When a pipe is passed to us, Louretta grabs it and takes a deep pull, but this time she doesn't choke. Instead, she French inhales slowly like she's been doing this shit for years.

Instant seduction kicks in, and she moves toward me and straddles me Indian style, wrapping her legs around me. The two Asian women hop into the tub, each one taking a seat behind Louretta and me. They begin massaging us as we fuck. Notice how I didn't say "make love" in that last sentence? That's because whenever there are two strangers buck naked with you in a horse trough that doubles as a bathtub, you're definitely *fucking* at that point.

In my head, I'm thinking that Louretta will immediately be freaked out by this, but instead, it's quite the opposite. This shit is going down. Eventually, we end up swapping Asian chicks. Louretta makes out with one like she's back in an Irish private school while the other one rides me, and Louretta is cool with it too.

As the hours pass, Louretta must get with ten different girls, as do I. Obviously, the Chinamen know I am their master, so nothing happens on the "other dude" tip with the missus. One dude does try to suck my dick, but I politely put the kibosh on it. He got caught up in the moment, and I understand.

Things become really hazy around 4 AM, when I see two more Asian women lead my steed into the barn. They begin to wash him with giant sponges; one girl even puts a hoof in her mouth. Look, I'm into some fucked up shit, but even I have to turn away at this point. Good for him and all that, but I don't need to see it.

As things take a turn for the bizarre, a blood-curdling scream rings out in the air. I can tell immediately that this is not a scream of pleasure. I run to the back of the barn, following the sounds of the screams. It's not *atypical* for someone to die during a drug-fueled orgy; a lot of people can't handle their shit. But this time no one is dead; someone is about to be born.

When I finally make my way to the source of the screaming, I stop in my tracks and look down at a nude woman in a trough of water, mixed with blood. It is Soon Lee, and she is having my baby.

One: this is the first and only time in orgy history that someone has physically gone into labor. Two: why do *I still have an erection*? Fight or flight, I guess. Adrenaline does some strange shit. With her screaming growing persistent, she grabs the sides of the trough with her hands and props her legs up over the sides. When she spots me, she looks up and briefly smiles.

"I knew you would be here for me and the baby," she says through gritted teeth.

"Yeah . . . I also don't want to fuck up this orgy, because we have a real good thing going on right now, so let's shoot this kid out. What do you say?"

She nods and begins to push. A Chinaman doctor runs over and puts a pipe in her mouth, with the opium acting as an epidural. She takes an enormous rip and exhales deeply. I look down and see the baby's head peeking out. He has my sweet hair. Within what seems like seconds after that first push, she goes from crowning to the full baby shooting out into the water like a dolphin birth. The doctor then bites off the umbilical cord and raises the child high above his head. He says a bunch of shit in Chinese, and everyone cheers. I well up as I look at the baby; he looks like an Asian me.

Everything else feels like a dream after that. I think I see my newborn baby riding through the barn on my horse at one point, but don't quote me on that. All I know is, I wake up the next morning with Louretta, back inside my house, in my own bathtub . . . full of doll parts and covered in someone else's blood. My Asian son's blood, to be exact. Best. Orgy. Ever.

Chapter Fifteen

IT TAKES ABOUT ONE HOUR UNTIL I AM RICH AGAIN

Remarkably, none of the Chinamen are hung over the next day. These motherfuckers are relentless. I nut up and take a Mexican shower—meaning I brush my teeth and put on a cowboy hat—before riding out with Daniel. Louretta waves at me as we leave. There is a strange calmness to her now, as if she has been to the other side and understands it. It scares the shit out of me. Daniel spits out a huge rope of tobacco juice on the ground and hands me a huge wad of chew from his shirt pocket. I upper-lip that shit and flick the reins on my steed.

"I saw you walk into the house last night covered in blood. What the hell happened at that party, Dad?"

"Let's just say you have a new brother."

"Wait, what?"

"I don't want to talk about it, Daniel, but it would be nice for you to learn Chinese."

We ride in silence the rest of the way into town. On Main Street, I see the two Schläger brothers that I smoked out yesterday already lined up in front of my new whorehouse. It's not as fancy as all the rest of the businesses in town, obviously, but the darker quality to it really adds to the mystery.

Daniel and I tie our horses up and step back in the street to take it all in. Painted on the sign above the entrance in big black letters are the words "St. James Place: Opium Den & Polite Whores." It is the first establishment in America that offers both opium *and* whores, so it is kind of a huge deal.

As I stand there looking up at the sign, a lion's pride washes over me. Samantha asks me to stand next to Daniel for a picture to properly mark this moment in history. I tell him I want a solo shot with my steed first, because I don't want people to think this is a father-and-son business. How would it look if I were selling whores with my son? It's not like we are fucking blacksmiths. Sam goes under a large blanket behind a camera set up on a large wooden tripod.

"One, two, three."

The bulb explodes in the air when the flash goes off, and it is really fucking dangerous. Samantha learns that firsthand when he steps out from underneath the blanket with his head smoking and his hair almost entirely burned off his scalp. He smiles and pats out a couple small flames of scorched hair.

"Are you okay, Sam?"

"Yes, I think so."

"Good, because I'm going to need one more; I think I was breathing out on that one. I need you to catch me on the breath *in*; it makes my pecs look bigger."

He nods in agreement and goes back under the blanket, proceeding to count me down again. Samantha sprints out from underneath the blanket completely engulfed in flames after the next one. He frantically runs toward the whorehouse, and I immediately kick him into a horse trough full of water so he won't light my place ablaze right before it opens. After making sure he is safely put out, I walk over to Daniel and look him square in the eyes.

"Daniel, you were my firstborn child that I actually took responsibility for, so I'd like you to be the first customer."

Daniel looks at me, touched. "Are you serious, Pa?"

"Yes. I obviously can't watch you fuck, though, because you're still at that awkward stage that verges on creepy. Also, you can't ever tell your mother about this. Got it?"

He laughs like a fourteen-year-old at a whorehouse, because he is. Catching himself being too excited, he steps back and firmly shakes my hand. Banging a whore is his last step toward becoming a man, and this is a really nice father-son moment. The nicest moment was obviously when he took sixty-three bullets for me, so I figure this is the least I can do to return the favor. As I walk him around the back, the two Schläger brothers who have been waiting out front start scratching their arms.

"Is there any chance you're going to open up early, Mr. Street James?" one of them asks.

I smile and point to Daniel as I say, "Gents, I'm gonna let my boy take the first hit off that wooden dick and then let him bang out one of the whores before we open to the public. It should be just a minute."

The other brother smiles. "That's lovely, man, I wish my father would have done that for me. Congratulations to you and your boy."

"Thank you. I tell you what, when I come out, I'll let you cut the ribbon as my 'real' first customers. How about that?"

"It would be an honor!"

Walking around back, I wave at my Chinamen neighbors who are feeding dead people to their pigs. Because I've picked this exact location, not only will people *not* be able to sneak in through the back because of my Asian connections, but customers will also be able to devour some delicious squirrel di on the way out. It's a win-win for everyone involved. I rap on the backdoor twice, and a beautiful Asian woman answers it in a silk kimono. She takes Daniel and me by the hands, leading us in.

The inside of the den is immaculate. Samantha and the boys did an unbelievable job recreating it to look exactly like the one I was at in China. Silk pillows cover the floors, surrounding a giant hookah in the middle of the room. Four more massive hookahs are set up underneath netting in each of the four corners of the joint. My own personal touch is a rice-wine room in the back where you can go if you want more privacy and pay a little extra.

The Asian woman sits Daniel down at the center hookah, already packed full of opium. I strike a match off the bottom of my boot and light the first honorary bowl inside my new establishment. Daniel chokes on the first hit, probably because of nerves, or due to the fact that he's smoking high-grade opium. Instead of laughing at him, I let him enjoy these last few minutes before his "prostitution virginity" is taken.

It's a big deal when you fuck your first prosty; it's not like having sex with a normal girl. A normal girl, you have to play coy and see what kind of positions they'll let you try, but with a hooker, the sky's the limit. You can ask for the fairy tale.*

"Have a good time, son," I say as I pat him on the back and walk out.

When I walk out the front door, I notice a small crowd has now gathered. I spot a man holding a soapbox and promptly take it from him, dumping all of his soap onto the ground before I jump on top of the box. Across the street, Mayor Van Buren curiously peeks his head out from behind a post. He holds his monocle up to his eye, examining the proceedings. I grab a cane from an elderly gentleman, who instantly falls over.

"Hear ye, hear ye, gentle townspeople. I am Saint James Street James, but you probably already knew that," I say as I motion down toward my cock with the cane.

"Today, I am here to open the first-ever opium den and polite whorehouse that has ever existed in America. No longer will you have to drink left-handed *liquor* with gold flakes floating in it. And gone are the days of having to put up with the sass of American whores. In here, you will be treated like gentlemen on a fine Oriental vacation. Plus, the girls don't speak English, so they can't say no!"

---

* "Fairy tale" means anal.

All of the men gathered roar with laughter. In the front, a man with a familiar face winks at me. As I look closer, I realize it's the fucking crazy gypsy woman dressed as an older businessman, complete with a long, fake white beard. I can't shake her. A part of me doesn't want to, either. It's sick, and it will come back to haunt me, but it makes my mind fucking dance.

"So come on in! Morning, noon, or night, our ladies will treat you right! The first time is on me! I'll also pay for it too."

The crowd erupts in laughter and rapturous applause. Two beautiful Asian girls in kimonos walk out holding a giant red ribbon and a pair of scissors. I ask the two Schläger brothers who have been waiting in line to cut the ribbon, and they run over like excited junkies.

"Samantha, one more picture please!" I implore him.

He pulls himself out of the trough he is cooling off his first-degree burns in, and gingerly walks over to the camera. *Flash!* Sam stumbles out from behind the curtain with his jeans burned almost completely off his body, and falls over facedown on the ground as I open the doors for business. A slew of gentlemen rush inside, including the crazy gypsy, who stops and grabs my penis as hard as she can. She whispers in my ear, "Don't you fucking dare say anything about me having a lady hole."

"Never," I say, still respecting her secret.

She grabs her fake dick and walks inside. Mayor Van Buren is still glaring at me from across the street, shaking his head in disgust. I tip my cowboy hat toward him and motion him over.

"Can I interest you in some opium and possibly a fine whore today, Mayor Van Buren? The first one is on me."

"No, thank you. I don't participate in those kinds of establishments."

"Your relatives do," I say, walking over to the camera, pulling out the sheet of glass containing the photograph. I hold it up to the sunlight so he can see the image of the Schläger brothers cutting the ribbon with me in between them. Mayor Van Buren fumes.

"Well, I'll have to see if the use of opium is in the book of laws or not," he threatens.

"I can assure you that there is no law *against* it."

"We'll see about that! Good day to you, sir!" he says as he storms off.

"Please fucketh off, sir!" I reply as I head straight over to Ron's printing-press office with my glass picture of the three of us. When I walk in, I see a man who appears to be Ron, but he looks different. This man is a little thinner and has a little more hair. I bird-dog a holster around his waist with a gun in it, so I proceed with caution and quietly draw my guns.

"Ron? Is that you? Say something, or I'll shoot your dick clean off your body."

"It's me! It's me! Please don't shoot my dick off my body; that's my biggest fear in life!"

His loose holster falls off onto the floor as he runs toward me. Same old gimpy Ron. In the light, I notice he's wearing a horrible toupee that is the same color and length of my hair. He's lost a few pounds, but he's still fat, the skinny-fat kind, with a lot of excess skin and zero definition. Truthfully, he should have just stayed fat.

"Is that gun even loaded, Ron?"

"No," he says sadly.

"Good. I wouldn't want you hurting yourself. Here, I need you to print this photograph of my grand opening and put it on the front page of tomorrow's paper."

"I have to run everything by the mayor now, Saint James."

"It's fine, the Schläger brothers are in the picture with me cutting the ribbon. We've buried the hatchet."

I hand him the glass plate, and he holds it up to the light, examining it. He seems surprised to see the Schlägers and me posing together. Ron takes it and carefully walks it over to the back of the shop, afraid of dropping it. From behind, I can see that he's even tried to flare his hair out like mine.

"Have you been growing your hair out for the last six years, Ron?"

He blushes, embarrassed that I said something. "Oh, you know, my wife asked me to grow it out. She likes it."

"You don't say? How is Sheila?"

"She's good, looks a lot older. You probably wouldn't recognize her, so there's no need to stop by ever again."

"Say hi to her for me, will you?"

"I sure won't. Is there anything else I can do for you today?"

"No, just run the article," I say as I walk out. I stop a couple steps before I hit the door and turn back toward him.

"Oh, and Ron, if Sheila *really* wants you to look like me, my gun belt has *two* holsters on it."

Shutting the door behind me, I take a few steps out into the street and see a steady stream of gentlemen walking into my new establishment. Sam runs up to me with a hat full of money and a forty-cent smile. Goddamn it, his teeth have gotten worse.

"Boss, we're making money hand over tits in there!"

I grab the hat and flip a few gold coins to him. He looks at me, puzzled.

"Take these and go buy yourself some new teeth. Also, get yourself a decent suit or a karate *gi*. Whatever the fuck you prefer to wear to greet the customers. I want you to run the place for me, and I'll be extending your cut by two percent. You've earned it."

His eyes well up with tears. "I don't know what to say."

"If you had manners, you'd say thank you."

"No, I don't know what to say, because I'm in so much pain. I can smell my own flesh cooking."

"Me too. Spray some cologne on it or something. I don't want you to scare any customers off."

I pat him hard on the back and walk through town with a new sense of confidence. I'm rich as fuck again, and it feels great. You see what happens when you use the hard work that someone else has done for you? That shit pays off. Time for Daddy to get suited up.

Kicking open the front doors, I strut into the Schläger Brothers Suit Store. Two different brothers stare at me suspiciously when I slam two gold coins down on the counter.

"I'll take two of your finest, boys. I'm a thirty-two waist, but be prepared to let the crotch way out."

"As the sailors say, we'll release the sheet, sir," one of them says while the other pours me a glass of Goldschläger.

"Come on, boys, you don't serve a man who orders two of your finest suits a glass of spring water. Where's the fucking whiskey? I know you got a bottle back there somewhere."

The two of them look at each other for a moment, then one of them finally walks to the back and comes out with a bottle of whiskey. We laugh as if they never killed my son, and I offer them cigars ...*laced with opium*. It's time to get the richest people in town hooked on my new product, so I have to infiltrate the rest of the brothers.

One by one, I smoke out every Schläger brother at each and every one of their businesses. I order up a shave, got some fresh meat from the butcher, buy some adult party supplies—you name it, I buy it. By the time I leave the last store, most of the brothers have already hung "Closed" signs on their doors and are heading over to party inside St. James Place. Game. Set. Match.

At the end of the day when I walk down Main Street with my new suit on, a fresh shave, and a large sack full of doorknobs, meat, and porn supplies over my shoulder, the townspeople look at me like they used to, with admiration mixed with fear. I can't even count how many women cock-gaze me. The six-year journey over to China was worth it. I am back on top.

When I mount my steed, I notice Daniel's horse is still tied up next to mine. That little son of a bitch is still at the den, probably going back for thirds at this point. Good for him; I know I would have. Why am I not going to the rice-wine room right now? After six years in China and four months of sixty-plus Chinamen living on my property with one outhouse, I just want to go home and be with my family. Totally kidding. I really just want to head home to put the feelers out to Louretta and see if she's down with another orgy. Maybe this could become a twice-a-week thing, or where she just watches sometimes—I'm not going to push it. I'll just see where it goes. Now that I'm rich again, I can at least ask.

I arrive home like jolly fucking St. Nick with a burlap sack full of gifts slung over my shoulder. Louretta and the kids greet me on the front porch, and I unload my bag of goodies for everyone. I pat my middle child on the head.

"I have a doorknob and a sturdy belt for you, Patrick."

"Dad, my name is Steve, and you look *really* high," he says.

I can't help but chuckle, remembering the first time I challenged my father too. "Well, look at you all full of shit and vinegar. Since you're such a big man now, I have one more thing for you."

Reaching into the bag, I pull out half a dead cow wrapped in a bloody sheet that I got from the butcher, and place it in his arms. Patrick struggles with it and falls over sideways on the porch. He looks up at me, helpless.

"Not so fucking big now, are you? Take that meat into the kitchen and divide it into chuck, rib, short loin, sirloin, round, shank, brisket, and flank steak."

"Dad, I don't know how to do any of that?"

"*Ohhhhhhh*, I thought you wanted to go by Mr. Know-It-All *Steve* who does shit on his own and has a fucking attitude about things. How's that working out, jackass?"

"Fine, I'll go by *Patrick*," he says, defeated.

"That's better. Now go and take that meat into the kitchen, and I'll slice it up like the man that you're not."

He gets up off the porch, dragging the huge piece of meat in behind him. Louretta walks over and kisses me like I'm a rich man again. There's a difference between how your wife kisses you when you have money and when you don't. This is an "I'll definitely be going down on you later, and I might even let you try your key in the backdoor" type of kiss. That orgy will definitely be going down now. She leans in and whispers into my ear, "You got anything in that sack for me?"

"The same set of nuts I've had on me my whole life. I also brought you back a gift." I reach into the bag and pull out an old-school wooden drill-do, which is a dildo made of mahogany attached to a bicycle frame consisting of only one wheel, a chain, and a set of foot pedals. If I'm being real with you, I don't even know how to fucking use it. The Schläger brothers are into some weird shit.

Louretta stares at it for a moment before finally asking, "Are those for *your* feet, or mine?"

"We can take turns. I'm starving, let's go make some dinner. Patrick, pick up the drill-do off the porch and put it in my bedroom!"

"It's Ste—never mind!"

We eat like whatever the opposite of Ethiopians are. So much so that I have to unzip my jeans and pull them down a little. It is a glorious night. Louretta and I drink goblets of rice wine, my kids laugh when I can't remember any of their names, and Daniel manages to make it home midway through the meal. When he stumbles in through the front door, his eyes are bloodshot red. He smells like stale sex and wet leather, a scent I've known for more than half my life.

IT TAKES ABOUT ONE HOUR UNTIL I AM RICH AGAIN

He hands me a fresh newspaper with the photo of the Schläger brothers and me cutting the ribbon on the front page. The caption reads: "Town's Elite Show Up for Grand Opening!" When I see it, I laugh like a schoolgirl with tuberculosis. Whoever said "Money can't buy you happiness" was obviously really fucking poor.

Chapter Sixteen

PEOPLE ARE STARTING TO HATE THE CHINESE. I GET IT.

ebruary 25, 1857—Two Years Later *Blam!* A big, greasy Schläger brother shoots his own brother dead in the middle of Main Street. Most of the patrons passing by don't even flinch, since it's become a daily occurrence. Neither do I, as I sit in front of St. James Place, calmly reading the newspaper. The fat Chinaman from the pig shack drags the dead body off the street and back down the alley, where he throws it to his eagerly awaiting swine.

Boom! A carriage crashes into another carriage at high speed right in front of me. Well, high speed for a fucking carriage. Samantha rolls out of it, laughing hysterically. You'd hardly recognize him. He now wears an ill-fitting suit and has big, fake white teeth, and his burnt hair has managed to grow back in patches. I'm surprised he didn't go with the karate gi, since I gave him a choice of either/or.

Here's what's been going on the last two years: opium, son. The Great White Dick. Poppy Sinclair. The Witches' Orgy. The Man with the Twisted Limp. O'Boogie. I have everyone smoking that shit. People became zombies, killing each other in the street. I was rich as fuck, so I didn't care. Was I still smoking it? You bet I was, because I can handle my shit like a grown man.

Mayor Van Buren tried in vain to pass legislation to ban opium the year before, but I smoked up all the senators before they went in to discuss it. They never even made it back out of chambers until the next day, and by then, they had totally forgotten about the whole thing. My product got so popular, I ran out for a couple months. I had to take half my Chinamen back to my farm to grow more. My property now has opium fields as far as the eye can see, and my kids all have their own horses, riding around the fields with shotguns protecting my crops.

Daniel, now sixteen, has grown into quite the man. It was his idea to make all the Chinamen strip buck naked before they harvest the opium every day, so they won't steal any. They're only allowed to put their clothes back on at the end of their shift after they spread their butt cheeks and cough for him. That little fucker is ruthless, and I love it. I pretty much just let him do whatever he wants, because he's fucking awesome.

Look, I know things aren't perfect in town right now. I'm not that delusional. People are getting sick of the Chinese, and I get it. Now that some of them have money, they have more freedom, which is not necessarily a good thing. They suck at driving carriages. They laugh quietly to themselves in an annoying way for no reason. They are always solving math problems. I guess that's just like a hobby to them?

Probably the most annoying thing, though, is that Samantha

won't stop taking pictures now. The other day we were at a diner for breakfast and he took a picture of his food. He actually ran across the street and grabbed that big-ass camera on the wooden tripod, pulled the curtain over himself, and took a picture of his fucking breakfast in the restaurant. Who does that shit?

I can't say anything to him, because he's still the only one who speaks Chinese and English, and I need a translator for everyone. Since he's had a little taste of power, he's also been dipping into the "pale-faced lady," trying to be like me. Obviously, he can't handle his shit the way I can, as evidenced by his latest carriage crash. Mayor Van Buren speed-walks across the street, his face red as hell. He points at Samantha and starts screaming.

"Goddamn it, Saint James, your Chinaman destroyed my carriage!"

"Just be grateful you weren't in it. Let's just take a step back, hold hands, and thank our Lord and savior Jesus Christ." I hold out my hand sarcastically for him to take. He slaps it away.

"Don't you give me your Jesus talk, you atheist!"

"Look, God is creating water right now." I point to Samantha, who is now pissing in the middle of the street.

"This is the second carriage of mine he's destroyed in the last week. I won't put up with it anymore! You've turned this town into a bunch of goddamn junkies!"

"As opposed to the respectful, incestuous rednecks you brought into town? And for what? Petty revenge over my old man numbing out your mom? Get over it. I've said this before and I'll say it again, fuck off, *Mayor*."

"I'm going to get the sheriff this time; we need to have some laws . . ."

As soon as the words come out of his mouth, we see the sheriff walking down the road minding his own business, when a tweaked-out Schläger brother, foaming at the mouth, runs out of my opium den holding a loaded peacemaker. He's talking nonsensically, but this time not in an endearing redneck way. The sheriff turns, but it's too late—*blam!*—the Schläger shoots him dead, before turning the gun on himself, blowing his own brains out.

I stand up and applaud as Mayor Van Buren looks on in shock. The fat Chinaman barrels out into the street again and grabs each of them one by one, throwing them over each shoulder. He laughs as he passes back by us.

"Hogs eat goo' today," he says with a smile.

I stop him and grab the sheriff's badge off his shirt and pin it to my suit. It looks nice on me, like it was meant to be. Mayor Van Buren shakes his head in disgust.

"You wanted law, you got law. I will protect and serve fine opium to the people!"

"You listen here, Saint James, I'm going to send a telegram for my father, the former president. He'll get the marshals out here!"

I stand up and quick-draw my gun, pressing it in his face. "You get that one-term slapdick father of yours down here, and all the fucking marshals you like. I own this fucking town now, and there's not a goddamn thing you can do about it. Isn't that right, Sam?"

Sam unleashes ten Chinese throwing stars into the wagon wheels of the mayor's busted-up carriage. The mayor looks at me, befuddled.

"No, the other thing, Sam."

Sam nods and pulls out a bottle of Goldschläger and smashes it against the side of the carriage. I then take a match, strike it off the sheriff's badge on my chest, and flick it on top of it. The entire carriage becomes engulfed in flames and immediately burns to the ground in a matter of seconds.

"Man, that was *really* fucking fast. I was not expecting that. That shit is *strong*," I note.

"You will rue the day you ever messed with me!"

I point over at Sam and say, "Just because he can't pronounce the word 'rule,' there's no need to inflict your racist pronunciation on him."

"No, I said 'rue,' which means to regret—forget it!"

Van Buren is so angry at this moment that he can't even speak. As he marches away, I walk over to his carriage to light a cigarette off a small remaining flame and I wonder if I've taken it too far. Maybe I've pressed my luck a little. That thought quickly vanishes and I remember looking down at my badge, thinking how cool it would be if someone blew me as the new sheriff. From behind a man taps my shoulder.

"How cool would it be if someone blew you as the new sheriff?"

"I was just—

"Thinking that? I know."

I turn and see the gypsy woman standing behind me, dressed in the sheriff's clothes that he just died in moments ago. His fresh blood is still on the shirt. She has also somehow shaved his mustache off and glued it to her face again.

Pulling out her gun, she whispers, "Come on, sheriff to sheriff, let's screw."

Why that seems right, I will never know. I pull her inside St. James Place, and that's what we do. We screw. Hard. In front of everyone. It creeps out a lot of people, and I lose a lot of customers and friends over it. That's what power does to you; it makes you think it's acceptable to fuck a woman dressed as a dude in front of *other* dudes. In reality, you need to keep that shit behind closed doors. I don't really give a shit which way you swing, that's just a general rule of thumb in a whorehouse if there's any cosplay involved.

This moment of carelessness is the beginning of the end for me. My rule, or *rue*, over the town has gotten too reckless. Things remain peaceful for a few days after I light the mayor's carriage on fire. I am an awesome sheriff, and there is hardly any crime. Seriously. Everyone is so afraid of pissing me off because they don't want me to blacklist them from my opium den that there isn't one single crime committed. Also, I am so high most of the time that I'm not even sure what really constitutes a *real* crime . . . until it happens to me.

About a week passes, and I'm sitting out in front of St. James Place reciting haiku and limericks, enjoying the fine smells of squirrel di wafting through the streets, when suddenly I hear collective screams from the townspeople. I stand up and see a man riding down Main Street toward me at a breakneck speed, with what appears to be a body dragging behind his horse. The man stops in front of me and flashes some sort of badge. It looks different from mine.

"Are you Saint James Street James?"

"I am *Sheriff* Street James, yes. Who the fuck are you?"

"I'm Marshal Mathers of the eighty-sixth district of the United States. I served under President Van Buren."

"Just say you were a *bottom*; you don't have to say you served *under* him."

He looks at me, confused. "This is a message from Mayor Van Buren: 'Your kid is dead. This is him.'"

I look down at the body, but it's almost unrecognizable. At closer glance, this could be anyone; it might not even be a human, that's how mangled it is at this point. I sit back down and continue my limericks aloud: "There was an old man from Peru."

Marshal Mathers becomes enraged. "This is your *son*, man. That we killed."

"If that's really one of my sons, what's his name?"

"Steve."

"Nope. I don't have a kid named Steve. Sorry, friend."

"He said you'd say that. So he told me to say 'Patrick.'"

Upon hearing this, I look down closer at the body, and that's when it sets in. It really is him.

"You motherfucker!" I draw my gun and shoot him in the chest, knocking him off his horse.

He hits the ground groaning in pain, trying to reach for his gun, but he can't. I stand over him, and his eyes widen as he says, "You don't shoot the messenger!"

"I just fucking did."

I unload the rest of my pistol into him. Breathing heavily and unable to speak, he bleeds out, dying in front of me. Out of my peripheral vision, I see another man on a horse riding in at the same speed. I quick-draw my other gun, but it's only Samantha. He looks completely distraught when he pulls up in front of me. As he gets closer, visible tears are streaming down his face.

"Sam, are you crying? What the fuck, bro?"

"Sorry, boss. They're dead. All of them are dead."

"Yeah, I know. Apparently Steve and Patrick are the same person."

"No, they set a fire. *Everyone* from the farm is dead. My family . . . and *yours*," Samantha wails, falling to his knees.

Have you ever gotten so angry that you start uncontrollably shaking and piss your pants? Typically it only happens to blind people when you fuck with their dogs, but it happens to me at this moment. I stand there frozen, violently shaking internally. After a long, steady release of urine, I scream toward the heavens and am finally able to concentrate. It's like I'm having an out-of-body experience, except this time I am inside myself as I watch myself from the outside. Sorry, I think that is the *exact* definition of an "out-of-body experience."

Adrenaline kicks in, and I pick Sam up by his belt loop, carrying him over to my steed. He's a fucking mess, and I know he can't ride in his condition. I hold him tightly against my horse and ride us home.

As we make our way through the forest, I can see fresh smoke billowing in the air from the grounds of my estate. Any doubts that Samantha is just really fucked up on opium and imagined both of our families burning in a fire are quickly erased. When we hit the edge of the tree line, my steed halts just in front of the slightly smoking grass where the fire has finally flamed out. As I survey the land, everything is gone. *Everything.*

PEOPLE ARE STARTING TO HATE THE CHINESE. I GET IT.

The opium fields: burned up. The rice paddies: nuked. My wife's garden: gonzo. My stables: smoldering ashes. The house: black char. My entire property looks like the inside of a wood-burning stove. I hop down with Samantha to see if there are any survivors.

My steed stays on the hill as we walk on foot through the charred ashes of the rice paddies. All that remain are burned, nude bodies serving as mere blackened grave sites amidst the landscape. Samantha walks over to their remains, trying to identify his relatives. Dental records don't exist yet, not that they would help the Chinese, obviously. Samantha hovers over a couple bodies and begins crying again. I can tell that he wants to be alone, so I leave him there to mourn and be with his people.

Walking back toward the house on my own, I pass by the stable, which is completely burned to the ground as well. The only thing I can make out is a large, black figure that is clearly Daniel's horse, which can mean only one thing: Daniel was home and probably didn't make it out alive. Goddamn it.

The house itself is almost entirely gone. A few smoldering boards from the foundation are all that is left. I can't even make out if there are bodies in the remains, because the house is so fucking massive. It has been reduced to a giant pile of used firewood, and it's clear everyone is dead. My entire family has now left this earth.

Before getting emotional, I peer over my shoulder to see if Sam is looking in my direction. When I see him curled up in the fetal position, wailing in the distance, I know I'm safe. If you do one thing in this life, never let another man see you cry. *Ever.* Just to be cautious, I turn my head and let out one solemn tear. The only tear of sorrow I will shed in my entire life. That's right: uno. One. Powerful. Motherfucking. Tear. In slow motion that PMT rolls off my cheek, extinguishing a tiny remaining flame on one of the smoldering boards beneath my feet. Deep down, I needed that tear to escape, so it wouldn't extinguish my fire within. Instead, I use that fire and turn it into white-hot, fuck-all revenge.

Seeing death this close really fucks people up on the inside . . . but not me. I know seeing some shit like this will harden me to anything I will ever see the rest of my life. This is the exact moment where I achieve old-man strength within.

My quiet inner rage is interrupted when I hear Samantha screaming for me. In the distance, I can see four US Marshals riding up to my property on horseback. I calmly walk toward them, knowing they will have to dismount their horses at the exact same place we did once they reach the charred ground.

"Saint James Street James, we have a warrant for your arrest. It's from the president," one of them says in a stern voice.

"For what?" I ask, stone-faced.

"Tax evasion. You did *not* pay the duty tax on your opium."

"When the fuck did that become a law?"

"1840, sir."

"Is that so? Well, as you can see I have no more opium; therefore there is nothing to tax. My fields mysteriously burned down."

"That's a shame. I hear that stuff is real flammable."

"Yeah. Apparently, people are too. We lost about sixty to seventy humans in the fire as well."

"I'm sorry to hear that. My condolences. Anyway, I got a telegram from Mayor Van Buren that says you've been running an opium den in town for the last two years, so you're going to need to pay up on that. The federal government will sort it out with you once we extradite you back to Washington."

"Sounds good. My condolences to you as well, by the way."

"For what?"

"On your impending deaths."

Full-on hysterical blindness has kicked in, and I become the ruthless motherfucker I was born to be. I quick-draw both pistols and blow all four marshals away. Standing over them, I calmly reload and fire two more rounds into each of them. Samantha stares at me as I walk over to my steed.

"Where are you going, boss?"

"There's only one person in this town who has the capability to send a telegram, and I'm going to pay him a visit."

"I can't leave them like this, I have to bury the bodies. It's a Chinese tradition."

"Luckily, I believe in cremation, so I'm all set. I'll be back to get you in a couple hours. Comb through these fields and see if you can scare up a couple unburned poppies for one last opium sesh. I'm going to need it after what I'm about to do."

He nods at me as I ride off . . . straight to fucking Ron's house. That gimpy motherfucker is the only one with a printing press capable of sending that telegram. I can't believe that son of a bitch sold me out again. Even my steed senses my anger, and this time, there's no need to dig my heels in; he's already at top speed.

As I near his house, I can see Ron watering his garden, enjoying his afternoon without a care in the world. That all changes the instant he hears my horse bearing down on him as we gallop closer. His eyes fill with panic, and he throws down his water bucket, running into his house as fast as he can, locking the doors behind him. My steed doesn't even attempt to stop as we arrive at the house. Instead he rides as close as he can to it and I jump off, crashing through the window, tackling Ron to the ground inside his own living room. He screams like the scared woman he is as I rip the gun out of his holster and begin to beat him with it.

Sheila comes running in from the bedroom; she's aged well, actually. To my surprise, she's also kind of dressed up, as if she has been expecting me to come over. I put Ron's gun to his head and squeeze the trigger. *Click.* Nothing. I knew it still wasn't loaded, but I wanted Sheila to know that Ron has been running around town holding a gun with no bullets in it.

At this point, I want to strip away any last bit of dignity and manhood that Ron is holding on to. I pick him up by his toupee, ripping it off his head. He screams as he flies backward into the kitchen. Looking down at the hairpiece, I can see yarn and chunks of his own skin still in it. He grabs his bleeding scalp.

"What the fuck? Did you sew this *into* your head, Ron?"

"Yes! I wanted—"

"To be like me. I know. Everyone does. Why did you send the fucking telegram, Ron? My entire family is dead!" I draw both my guns.

"Not your *entire* family," an unfamiliar voice says behind me.

I quickly turn around and see an eight-year-old boy who looks exactly like me standing by the stairs. Sheila smiles and puts her arm around him. I'm completely dumbfounded and at a loss for words at this moment.

"This is your son. Saint James Street James Junior."

"I don't know what's more confusing, the fact that I have a son I've never met, or the fact that you named him entirely after me and made Ron raise him?"

"That's why I sent the telegram, Saint James. Do you know how hard it is raising a son that looks exactly like the man your wife slept with?"

"Shut the fuck up, Ron. It's not as hard as losing your entire family in a house fire, so don't even give me that bullshit."

On the one hand, I *really* want to kill Ron. On the other, I'm not going to raise the goddamn kid, and it will be more painful if Ron has to do it for the rest of his life. Having that constant reminder every single day will be mentally debilitating, but Ron still needs to pay for what he did. I take out a cigarette and hand it to the young me.

"Here, go take Ron's horse down by the river and have a smoke. Come back in a half hour."

"Okay, Dad," he says with a smile as he scampers outside.

"Did you hear that, Ron? He called me *Dad*. That's a feeling that you never deserve to have. Stand up and pull your pants down."

He looks up at me, confused. "What?"

"Pull down your fucking pants, Ron!"

He puts his hands up, pleading with me to stop. "Saint James, please!"

I cock both my pistols and say, "Do it now."

"Okay, okay," he says as he slowly pulls his pants down around his ankles.

"Underwear too, Ron."

"Oh no, please don't do this! Please!"

"I'm sure that's what my wife and kids said. *Pull them down*."

Ron starts sobbing uncontrollably as he begins to tug on his underwear, pulling them down past his knees. I walk over to Sheila, grab the back of her head, and kiss her like she's the last woman on earth as Ron watches. Satisfied that I have delivered the most passionate kiss she will ever receive in her entire life, I turn and shoot Ron's dick clean off his body. It hits the floor with the sound of a wet pickle escaping a jar.

His scream is delayed five seconds, obviously from the shock he's in. Once his brain registers what has just occurred, he falls to his knees in agonizing pain, screaming and holding his crotch. I put my gun back in my holster and walk toward the door, stopping in the door frame to turn back once more to Sheila.

"Use Ron as an example of who you shouldn't raise our son to be like, Sheila."

Sheila wipes away her tears and shakes her head. She says, "I will. Where are you going?"

"I don't know. Maybe to Europe to paint or write poetry for a few years."

"*Really?*"

"No. I'm going to kill every last motherfucker who did this to my family. Make a tourniquet and get the stepdad to a doctor. Oh, and Ron, you're not a starfish, so that thing isn't growing back. Know that this happened to you because of the decisions you made to be a bitch in this life."

Night has fallen on the ride back over to my property. When I arrive, I can see Samantha down by the river, lighting paper Chinese lanterns, one for every family member that he lost. One by one he slowly releases them into the water, wistfully watching them float away. Tears roll down his face, as he stands there motionless. I notice he has saved seven lanterns for me. Even though I'm not really into that shit, the gesture is appreciated, so I join him and begin to light them anyway and release them downstream as well. Just as I'm about to light the last one, a foot suddenly stomps down on it, smashing it to pieces.

"No need to be lighting that last one," a gravelly voice says.

I draw my guns and look up. It's Daniel. He's burned to shit, but he's still alive. This motherfucker will not die. I stand up and hug him as hard as I can, and he screams in pain.

"Dad, I'm covered in third-degree burns! Stop!"

"Sorry, I just—it's amazing that you're alive. You really *won't* die. It's truly remarkable."

"Fuck you, man. I need to go sit in the river for an hour."

He takes off the remainder of his burnt clothes and heads out into the water. My heart is filled with joy and relief as I watch the smoke rising off him as he wades out in the river. I remember staring at his innocent face, thinking to myself, "Sweet Jesus, how are three men going to make it back into town on one horse? Would it be rude to ask Sam to walk back?" In the end, I decide it won't. It is only six miles, and it probably will give him time to think.

Chapter Seventeen

TIME TO KILL EVERYONE IN SIGHT . . . RELAX, THEY DESERVE IT

There comes a time in every man's life where he has a breaking point. A time where mentally, you just can't take it anymore. Something snaps inside your soul. For me, that time comes when I step into my opium den later that night and see my prized hookah busted to shit. When I see it shattered in the middle of the room, I *really* lose it. I fall to the ground, holding its remains. It truly feels as if I have just lost yet another family member. Maybe even a little worse.

My voice starts to shake, but I manage to get out the words, "Who did this?"

"Mallshows and Mayo Van Bulen," one of my prized Asian whores answers.

"Does anyone have *anything* to get high with? All my opium fields got burned down."

Samantha's old, creepy uncle hobbles forward. His pube beard that he glued to his face is somehow still mostly intact. He hikes up his robe, revealing a wooden leg. Without hesitation he rips off the leg and unscrews the back of it by the ankle. A hush of silence falls over the room, and when a strand of hair falls off his face, you can hear that pube drop.

He opens up a secret compartment inside the leg, revealing an old opium pipe stashed away as if it were a rare violin inside a case. It has a long porcelain stem with floral and bird motifs hand-painted on it. Every Asian man bows. Daniel removes his hat. Samantha kneels down. Every whore in the room disrobes and gets on all fours.

To say that this pipe is simply "beautiful" does not do it justice. No, this piece is majestic. It is the most perfect thing I have ever held in my hands, besides my own dick. Holding something like this truly happens only once in a lifetime.

He puts the pipe in my mouth and forcefully strikes his wooden leg on the floor, creating a small flame with his peg leg. Wood on wood. Old-school shit. He lights my bowl with the wooden toe section, and I inhale the purest, cleanest hit of *lachryma papaveris* ever imaginable. Yeah, the shit is so good I have to say it in Latin.

Right as I am about to exhale, the front doors suddenly fly open. I quick-draw my guns and turn to see Ron, now ghastly pale and shivering. He's standing there with his toupee half heartedly glued back onto his head and blood covering the front of his jeans where his crotch is. I notice him clutching a piece of paper in his hand.

"Jesus, Ron, I told Sheila to put a tourniquet on that thing!"

"I got it sewed back on. Doc says I will never achieve a full erection, but I might be able to get it to go from 6:00 to 8:45 someday," he says with hope.

"That's great, Ron. What the fuck do you want? I'm kind of in the middle of something here."

"I got a telegram that's supposed to go to Mayor Van Buren. It's from the US Marshals office. They're sending a hundred marshals here to get you tonight. *Dead or alive.*"

"Why are you telling me this?"

"I feel bad for being a gimp all these years. You did what any *real* man would do in the situations I left your wife and kids in repeatedly, and I just want to say I'm sorry." Ron folds his hands and looks down at the floor, still not wanting to make direct eye contact with me.

"And I'm sorry for blasting your dick off. That was a level I was not expecting to go to, but it happened. I sincerely do hope those stitches take and you're able to get it to 8:45 again one day. Now get the hell out of here and take care of my kid who looks exactly like me, will you?" I finally smile at Ron for the first time ever.

"I will."

"Don't go letting him come looking for me one day."

"Okay," he says, as he forces a smile and limps out.

The entire room stares at me in silence as I finally exhale that hit I took before Ron came in. As I look at all those Asian faces staring back at me, everything becomes so clear. My rage quiets within, and I am able to control it. In this moment of clarity I realize that these beautiful people have been through enough. My war should not become *their* war.

"Samantha, take your people and get out of town. I don't want to put you and your family at further risk."

Samantha looks at me, touched. "No, boss, I battle with you. We've been through too much together. You are the reason I have teeth."

"I know, but you need to get the rest of your family out of here safely. Daniel will take you."

Daniel throws up his hands. "What? Dad, no way. I'm staying here with you."

"Daniel, you've almost died *twice*. You're the only one I have left. I'm not going to lose you for what I think will be a third time. I can't take that again."

"But Dad, that's too many marshals for you to take on. You need me."

"What I *need* is for you to take Samantha and his family out of here. Head as far east as you possibly can. I'll find you guys."

Daniel hangs his head before muttering, "Okay." His eyes well up, and I motion him over and hug him.

Just as we break the embrace I say to him forcefully, "You have to go right now."

He nods, knowing that it's for the best. I walk them out and help Sam squeeze his thirty remaining family members into the back of a small covered wagon. He pulls down the cover and attempts a smile, knowing this is it. Our friendship is at another crossroads. We shake hands as he climbs up front with Daniel.

"There's still room in the wagon," he says.

I shake my head as I look inside and see Sam's relatives piled on top of each other three-deep. "No, I have to stay and fight, or else they'll just be chasing me forever. Plus, this looks really uncomfortable."

"Okay. By the way, there's a cellar door underneath the floorboards. It will buy you some time if they burn the place down," Sam says.

"Then what?"

"Then they'll probably shoot you after that, but it's better than burning to death. No offense, Daniel."

Daniel lights a cigarette off his own skin. "None taken. Asshole."

"Thanks. I'll see you guys soon . . . I hope."

He whips the reins on a horse that is definitely not mine. I love my family and friends, but no one is taking my fucking steed. Daniel smiles and waves good-bye with a hand-sewn queef mitten now on his hand. "That SOB banged one of my whores? Awesome," I think. What a championship exit. Goddamn it, I love that kid.

When I walk back inside I notice the front door is slightly cracked open. I draw my pistols and slowly approach the front of the opium den. I hear a floorboard creak as I peer out from behind a large wooden beam. The coast seems clear, so I walk out into the center of the den, when out of nowhere a marshal jumps down off a beam in the ceiling and shoots me in the shoulder. I fall to the ground hard.

"Saint James Street James, you're wanted for murder. You killed my—"

Before he can finish his sentence, I roll over on my back and unload both my pistols into his body. He falls to the floor, gasping for breath. I slowly get up and walk over to his sprawled-out, bleeding body. Up close, I realize it's not a marshal at all. It's the fucking gypsy woman.

Her eyes widen as she says, "You . . . killed . . . my . . . *pussy.*"

"Why did you do this to me?"

"This is how it was supposed to end. Find another man for me."

And with that last and final statement, she passes, still staring straight at me like a fucking psychopath. I kick her in the ribs to make sure she's really fucking dead. She's gone for good, but I can't have her staring at me like this. I try to close her eyes by hand, but they still won't go down. Digging into my pockets, I pull out a couple loose nickels and place them over her eyelids. It does no good, they pop right back open. Finally, I just roll her over on her stomach so she's facedown.

I rip down a silk curtain outside the rice-wine room and wrap it around the fresh hole in my shoulder. My steed neighs loudly out front, and I suddenly hear the sounds of hooves sprinting outside, approaching the den. I quickly run over to the front door to let him in before slamming it shut.

Through the window I can see a hundred marshals pull up on horseback. Some of them are holding torches, others shotguns, and one of them has two rake heads tied to his arms with yarn. I'm at a loss for the last dude. Mayor Van Buren walks out and stands next to them with a huge smile on his face.

"Saint James Street James, we got a warrant for your arrest. You can either come out peacefully, or we can burn the place down. It's up to you."

"Let me think it over."

"You're lucky we're even giving you the option. Your wife and kids didn't even know it was coming."

"I'm going to kill you in the most fucked up way I can possibly think of, Van Buren!"

I grab the body of the gypsy and pull her cowboy hat down over her face, dragging her over to the front door. With my leg, I pull the door open and use my free arm to put my gun to her head. Every single marshal has his guns trained at me. The one dude with the rake heads tied to his arms just spins in a circle, further confusing me.

"You burn this place down, I kill this marshal first. You understand me?"

The gypsy's creepy eyes are still open as I cock the gun. The marshals hold their fire, trying to figure out who it is. Satisfied that I've given them just enough of a glance to keep them at bay, I quickly walk back in and slam the door behind me. Mayor Van Buren huddles up with a couple of the marshals, and they have a small conference. After a few moments, he shakes his head and looks back toward me.

"All right, what do you want for the marshal, Saint James?"

"I want to see my son one last time. Dig him up and bring him here."

Mayor Van Buren and the rest of the marshals laugh. "Which one?"

"The one your boys dipped in gold. Totally Fucking Mexico. You bring him here, and I'll come out peacefully. I want to see my boy."

Mayor Van Buren takes a moment and confers with the marshals. They all nod their head in unison. "You got a deal."

"Deal," I say as I quickly pull the silk curtains shut to cover the window. I know goddamn well they won't be able to lift him, and it will buy me some time . . . unless they figure out that the gypsy isn't one of theirs. I walk to the back of the den to cover those windows as well, and I see that there are a few marshals in the alley, maybe ten or so. I make a blowjob motion toward them before slamming the curtains shut.

Knowing that my time is fleeting, I drop down to the floor on all fours and start tossing the throw pillows, searching for the mystery door. I slide my hands across the floor a few minutes before finally stumbling upon something. Cautiously, I place my hand over the door, examining it. I lean down and hear whispering coming from below, so I put my ear on top of the door. It sounds like people laughing. Maybe Samantha forgot some of his relatives.

As I pull open the cellar door and walk down a creaky set of stairs, a hush falls over the room. There's barely any light, except from tiny flames underneath a small cauldron that's lit in the middle of the basement. When I hit the last stair, I see about fifteen Native Americans standing there in loincloths, aiming bows and arrows at me. A large white buffalo is lying on the ground next to them. I hold up my hands and squint, trying to make out their faces.

"Stop right there, white man," an Indian voice says.

"I don't mean to bother you. I own the whorehouse upstairs," I say as I make a jack-off gesture.

"Shit, Saint James, we almost scalped your ass! Put the bows down, boys." The other Indians oblige and put down their bows and arrows. It's Manuel! Thank Christ. We embrace in a long hug. I can't tell you how relieved I am to see this motherfucker right now.

"Look who's pretending to be Indian, you son of a bitch! By the way, you look terrible in a loincloth."

"Fuck you," he says as he laughs.

No lie, he really does look awful in a loincloth. He's super soft and out of shape, not like the ripped Indians you see in the old black-and-white drawings in schoolbooks. Realizing his nude dong is pressed against my leg, I break out into a weird Indian handshake that I don't know.

"What's up with the white buffalo?"

"Oh, it has a pigment disease. Don't worry, there's not like a hidden Indian meaning to it or anything."

As the smoke starts to clear, I can see the eldest Indian stirring something in the cauldron with an old wooden boat oar. "What the fuck are you guys doing down here?"

"Samantha lets us hide out in here and make ayahuasca during the day. The marshals want all the Indians dead in this area, or 'moved,' as white people conveniently call it. We can only go out in a group at night when it's dark enough that we can pass for Mexicans."

"Still playing that Mexican card, huh? Well, if it's any consolation, they want me dead right now too. There's a hundred of them outside surrounding the place."

"Wait, you have a hundred marshals out there waiting for you? Like, *right now*?"

"Yeah, I even got a fake hostage upstairs, which will probably buy me another hour or so. That is, until they figure out it's not really one of them and they burn this place to the ground. You want to pour me a bowl of that shit?"

"Asshole, that means we can't get out of here either. If they set this place on fire, we'll burn with you!"

"Yeah, that seems to be the sitch. Can you pour me a bowl? I hate saying things twice."

"Goddamn it, Saint James, this is some serious shit!"

Manny shakes his head and picks up a hollowed-out armadillo shell. He dips it inside the cauldron and hands me a bowl of ayahuasca tea as I join the circle with the rest of the Indians. We all look at one another and drink in unison. As soon as the bitter tea hits my throat, I can feel it slowly racing through my veins. The Indians feel it as well, and stare at each other intensely. I look over at Manuel, who pours a shellful into the buffalo's mouth.

"Is that thing going to be cool on that?" I ask.

"Are *we*?" he retorts as both of us laugh. This special bond between a white man and a magical Indian is interrupted by a marshal screaming outside.

"Saint James! We got your boy! You have two minutes to come out with your hands up, or we burn the place down!"

What the fuck? This can't be, it's only been like an hour or so. I run up the stairs and peek out the curtain. The marshals pry open a coffin and begin to pull the top of his gold statue out, trying to stand it upright. Shit, man, these marshals are playing for keeps. I walk back down the stairs and salute everyone farewell.

"This is the end of the line, boys. I appreciate your hospitality."

"No," says the eldest Indian stirring the cauldron. Everyone turns and looks at him. "I am the acting chief of this tribe, and if you burn, we burn with you."

He holds up his hand and sticks it into the flames underneath the cauldron, palm-side down. That motherfucker never breaks eye contact with me as his skin melts. I'm not going to do that shit, but it is awesome to see someone else do it. With the smell of burning flesh resonating through the air, he smiles and says, "Are you ready to fly with the sea of wingless birds?"

Without hesitation, or knowing what the fuck he is talking about, I reply, "I am."

He closes his eyes and begins chanting in a deep, low, resonating voice. The other Indians close their eyes and join in as well. The old chief then pulls a battered wooden box from behind him. He carefully lifts the top, revealing twenty live rattlesnakes. He motions for me to grab a snake with my bare hands. I'm so fucking high on ayahuasca that I don't even flinch as I stick my hand in.

"Now, slowly apply pressure to the neck of the snake with four fingers and ease your thumb upward. When he exposes his fangs, squeeze your thumb down on his head, closing his mouth gently."

I do exactly as told. The rattlesnake shakes his tail wildly as milky white venom begins to slowly seep from his mouth. Holy shit, this is intense.

"I want each of you to turn to the man next to you and draw a spirit animal on each other's face in rattlesnake venom," the chief says in a stern voice.

Manuel turns to me, and I close my eyes. He begins rubbing the closed mouth of the rattlesnake against my face in a controlled manner. I can feel the warm venom slowly sinking into my cheeks. It burns like a motherfucker with an intensity that makes you want to kill someone. When he finishes, I open my eyes and do the same to him.

The old chief smiles and says, "On the count of three, I want you to tell the other person what you drew. One. Two. Three."

"A bald eagle," Manuel and I say in unison.

The chief nods and says, "You are ready. Let's go kill some white people."

Suddenly, we hear the sounds of Goldschläger bottles crashing through the windows of my opium den, followed by the unmistakable smell of smoke. The den immediately goes up in flames. I hear my steed upstairs neighing loudly, and I know it's go time. The old chief takes our rattlesnakes and puts them back in the box.

With my face burning, I instinctively take off my shirt to become one of the Indians. One by one we head up the stairs as the flames grow higher. I hop up on my steed and look down at Manuel, who is now riding the white buffalo up from the cellar.

The Indians fall in behind him, pulling out hatchets attached to their calves. They give the go-ahead signal to Manuel, who slaps the buffalo hard on the ass. It takes off like a rocket, crashing through the front door and out into the street. The marshals are paralyzed with fear as it knocks a few of them down off their horses. That guy with the rakes tied to his arms tries to spin into the animal, swinging at it wildly. Obviously, the buffalo tramples him to death in brutal fashion. That really is the first guy I wanted to see die, just because of his own stupidity.

In a state of bewilderment, the other marshals pivot hard on their horses in mass confusion, unable to get a clean shot off at him.

An albino buffalo sighting is a rarity anyway, let alone one busting out of a fake hostage situation after you set an opium den on fire. I whip the reins of my steed, and he takes off running through the whorehouse at full speed, shattering through the window, out onto Main Street. The Indians immediately sprint out behind us and start throwing hatchets at the marshals.

There's so much chaos going on that the marshals fumble with their weapons, not knowing where to shoot. I draw my guns and start blasting the shit out of people. One by one, marshals begin to hit the ground, splattered in blood, dead as fuck.

Amidst the confusion, I hear a loud war cry from the roof, where I see the old chief standing. He throws the wooden box full of rattlesnakes high in the air down toward the marshals. The snakes spill out everywhere when the box crashes to the ground, spooking the marshals' horses, causing them to buck them off. Some of their horses fall on top of them on the ground, crushing their legs. The rest of the Indians pounce and begin scalping them one by one. Blood flies everywhere. It's graphic as shit, even more so when you're on drugs.

Indians don't give a fuck, either. Real talk, they would have killed all of us white men if it weren't for the invention of muskets. Muskets changed the game; we had them, and they didn't. Simple as that. Watching them kill right now, I realize and appreciate how hardcore these motherfuckers are. Plus, the ayahuasca heightens your awareness, and you're really able to hone in and take souls. I can't recommend it enough when you're in a "kill-or-be-killed" situation.

With the sounds of horses approaching from behind, I spin my steed around in their direction. The marshals who were stationed out back suddenly come flying around the corner on horses with their guns drawn, aimed square at me. I fire my pistols, but they're out of bullets. As I quickly try and reload, I realize it's too late. They have the drop on me. All ten marshals smile.

"Good-bye, Saint James Street James," one of them says.

"I'm about to go Totally Fucking Mexico!" a voice screams out.

The marshals turn toward the voice, where the statue of Totally Fucking Mexico has come to life—but it's not him. It's Daniel, who has painted himself gold. The realism is frightening, and Daniel exploits the stunned marshals, who hesitate to fire. He pulls out his pistols and begins shooting at the marshals as he runs out in front of me.

I scream out to him, "Daniel! No!"

He manages to take out four or five marshals before they regain their senses. All at once they fire in unison, peppering him with hot lead. After he's hit with what seems like more than a hundred rounds, I see massive amounts of blood pouring out of his body. With the few bullets I was able to jam into my guns, I'm able to kill the remaining marshals. I quickly dismount my steed and run over to Daniel, as his near-lifeless body falls to the ground.

"Daniel, why did you do this?"

"I just wanted to prove myself to you, Dad."

"You've proven yourself like three times. More than any father could ever ask of his son. Also, that paint job is un-fucking-believable. You look just like him. He would be proud."

"Thanks, Dad."

"Out of curiosity, how did you know to run home and do this?"

"I'm a Street James. We think alike," he says as he tries to smile and violently coughs up blood.

"This probably isn't the time, but this is the last thing I would have thought to do."

"Yeah, but you probably wouldn't have thought about doing *this* either."

He reaches into his pocket and pulls out the queef mitten, wrapping it around my hand. I smile and begin to well up.

"I think I see Ma."

"Run to her, Daniel," I say, realizing there's nothing I can do. He's bleeding too much and he's about to die. As a father, I comfort him as much as I can, as he nods his head gently and closes his eyes. I hold him in my arms and look up toward the sky as the Indians pounce on the dead marshals and scalp the shit out of them. When they finish, the Indians walk over and rub their fingers in Daniel's blood and wipe them underneath their eyes out of respect for this fallen warrior.

As I sit with his head in my lap, I hear a set of saloon doors swing open behind me from across the street. Before I can turn to see who it is, I'm shot in the other shoulder. What are the fucking chances? I look back and see Mayor Van Buren firing a small derringer at me like a fucking woman. Glancing down at my shoulder, I'm more pissed off than anything. Of course this little motherfucker has a derringer.

With fear in his voice, he screams out at me, "Fuck you, Saint James! I'll kill you just like I did the rest of your family!"

He empties the last two shots of his little, tiny gun at me, missing wildly. Running like a scorned woman, he jumps on his horse and rides off. When I stand up and cock my pistols, taking aim at him, a hand reaches over and grabs my arm firmly. It's old-man strength. I don't even have to look over to know that it's the chief.

Completely covered in marshals' blood from neck to nuts, he looks me directly in the eyes and says, "No gun. When a man takes another man's entire family, that man needs to feel his life being taken from him by the hands of the man he has taken from."

"Thank you, wise Chief. The word 'man' was used *a lot* in that last sentence, but I understood it." He gives me two small hatchets, and in return, I hand him my guns.

"Trust your instincts, and the spirit world will guide you into a cloud through time and space, which will in turn lead you to the other world, where you will meet a man with no face who cannot eat—"

"I hate to cut you off, but the mayor is getting away, and I have no idea what the fuck you're saying right now. I should go."

The old chief smiles, "Forgive me, the ayahuasca has just taken ahold of me. I have said too much weird shit."

The fact that it's now just kicking in is amazing. I'm astonished at the chief's tolerance for hallucinogens. He takes my hands and squeezes them around the hatchets, before circling the dead marshals, chanting. I tuck the hatchets in the back of my jeans and ride off on my steed like never before. It feels like I'm riding on Pegasus as I trail the mayor along the river.

The moon is now out and full as fuck, no doubt having my back.

I'm able to see this chubby little coward's shadow perfectly bouncing up and down on his horse along the edge of the water. I look up at the big guy, who winks at me again, and I swear to God, the moon mouths the words, "Fuck. That. Dude. Up."

You bet your ass, moon. With my horse now at top speed, I'm just a few lengths from him. Bearing down hard, I'm finally able to get close to him. I leap from my steed, knocking the mayor off his horse in midair, just as we hit the edge of a cliff and plunge over a waterfall.

Somehow, I'm able to grab him around the neck as we flail through the air. I put him firmly in a chokehold and punch him in the face with my other arm as we descend. Directly in front of me I see my steed kicking the mayor's horse in the face on the way down as well. The four of us plunge into the water forty feet below with unspeakable force.

I rise out of the water like a great white sensing a kill. My steed pops up and swims over to land, shaking off the jump like a fucking boss. Down the river fifty yards or so, I see Van Buren's horse floating facedown, dead. The current washes the massive body downstream, but the mayor is nowhere in sight.

I dive back down underwater, and I'm able to spot him with the bright light of the moon. Miraculously, he's still alive; his suit jacket is caught on a rock. He flails his arms and legs, struggling for breath. I'm going to go ahead and answer your question, fuck no I'm not going to let him drown, *because he deserves worse.* He deserves to see my eyes as I kill him. Maybe even my dick. Relax, it's not gay, it's just a show of one male being superior to and dominant over another male.

Grabbing the back of his collar, I drag him out of the water and onto shore. As he gasps for breath on land, I pick him up and choke-slam that motherfucker to the ground. He vomits out all of the water in his lungs. Studying my prey, I slowly circle him and pull both hatchets out of the back of my jeans. His eyes widen in terror as I begin to unzip my pants. I just told you I was going to do that, so why the fuck are you shocked? As I pull off my jeans, he tries to squirm away, grabbing at reeds of grass. Now butt-ass naked, I kick him in the ribs and he rolls around weeping, a lot like Ron used to.

"Please don't kill me! Please don't kill—why the hell are you *naked*?"

"Because I want you to know that a *man* killed you. A real man, not some fucking pussy who burned down someone's house and killed their entire family while they were helpless. This is how a real man kills another man when he wants to take him out of this world."

Leaping on top of him, I pin his arms down with my knees, letting my entire dick and balls hang inches from his face. With a mighty force, I swing down hard with both my hatchets, chopping off each of his hands simultaneously. He screams in agony.

I pick his right hand up off the ground and stuff it in his own mouth, muffling his cries. We lock eyes, and I turn him over on his stomach, pulling down his trousers as he tries to scream. I think about raping him, but after what he did to my family, I need to go *further*. This time I want to do something so fucked up, that it will fuck up whoever finds him as well, knowing that this dead man did something horrific to deserve this.

That's when I make the decision to reach over and pick up his bloody chopped-off left hand . . . *and jam it up his own ass.* His eyes almost pop out of his head as he waves his bloody stumps around in violent protest, while kicking his legs wildly. I can hear the crunching of his own bones echoing throughout the land as he bites down on the hand in his mouth. He tries to move, but he can't do shit, unable to do anything but sit there with his whole goddamn hand up his own ass. Fuck him.

When I finally decide he has had enough and it is time to end his life, I take a hard seat down on his back. I pull his head close to me and look up at the moon for approval to scalp him. The moon nods and gives me the final go-ahead.

I take a deep breath and roar like the old chief as I place my hatchet to his scalp. When my blade pierces through the top of his brain, ending his life, I hear the screams of a thousand wolves howling with delight. A bald eagle flies down and lands in front of me. We make eye contact as the Indian spirit courses through my veins. I have become one of them.

Satisfied with my kill, I stand up and slap Van Buren's scalp against my dong, before casually tossing it into the river, further asserting my manhood and dominance. After a full ten minutes of staring at my fully flexed physique reflecting off the water, I finally walk over to my steed and ride off butt-ass naked into the moonlight. I don't know where I am going next, and I don't fucking care. In this moment, I feel a sense of peace knowing that the only two things I need in this cold, dark world are between my legs: my steed, and my dick and balls.

Congratulations, you've just completed the best book you've ever read in your entire life. Oh, were you hoping I was going to kill myself now? Like I said, I've lived a long life, so that might take a while. In the meantime, go stare at yourself in the mirror and dream about being me until the next one comes out.